GUARDIAN OF THE FIREFLIES

BARBARA GNECCHI

©2022 Barbara Gnecchi
Guardian of the fireflies
All rights reserved

Cover by Rapolas Vilunas
Layout by Giorgia Ragona
Illustrations by Foxyliam

ISBN 9798412632018
http://www.wirresorts.com/

For Marco and Guia

In the mists of time, its name was Tambapanni, but the Greek sailors, unable to pronounce it, called it Tabrobane. "The island of hyacinth and ruby".

For the Persians, it was "The land of happiness and fantastic treasures".

Then the Arabs came and called the island Serendib, from which the English word "serendipity" originates, the mood of those who make casual pleasant discoveries. However, for the Sinhalese, it is simply Sri Lanka.

For Indians, it is "La Tear", ". For Marco Polo, it was "The most beautiful island in the world".

For the Portuguese, it is "Zelan, the lion island", from which the name Ceylon originates, but for the Sinhalese, it is simply Sri Lanka.

Few places on Earth have a cultural, historical, artistic and naturalistic abundance so vast that it cannot be contained in such a small territory...

CHAPTER 1

If it's true, as they say, that for better or for worse everything starts from the foundations, my story starts right here.

My lifelong friend Mars and I had thought about our life projects many times: the last few years had been really tough, packed with work and we had often fantasised about the perfect place to design something unique to crown our careers as architects.

We had met more than ten years earlier in Milan, in the then fervent city of design, two young creatives with plenty of motivation and drive.

We found ourselves working together where a creative and worldly Milan was at its best. We had frequented the highest levels of Italian architecture and design as an unlikely couple. Back then, in our environment, everyone used to call us the "ladies of design". I was very different compared to all my friends, always needing to run away, change and experiment; he was handsome and gay, almost uniquely creative and brilliant. We spent our social evenings "stealing" the best-looking boys from each other, gossiping about uptight ladies and dreaming.

We soon started traveling together to find inspiration in work as well, and so we set off on our first trip to India, full of expectations. We immediately felt at home, walking through the ramshackle suburbs of Dheli, mingling with the crowds in Choudi Chouk, the most infamous district in the city, adorning ourselves with flower necklaces and pretending to be two film stars.

We were dazzled by the beauty of the women wearing saris from the villages in Rajasthan, so dressing ourselves in saris and mingling with the dancing crowds on the days of Diwali, sprinkling coloured powders over ourselves during Holi and sleeping in the palaces of the Maraja, where Mars pretended to be one of them, we spent one of the best periods in our lives.

Fascinated by the Indian ambience, we decided to head off to Nepal together to see the sunrise on Annapurna and pray in front of the burning pyres on the Katmandu river. Mars disappeared for two days that time, bewitched by the Shadu;

he came back dressed like them and remained that way for a number of days.

We were inspired by the wonders of Baktapur, the precious wood carvings of Nepalese windows and the majesty of the red temples of Patan. We let ourselves become intoxicated by everything we saw, savouring its deeper meaning. It was never enough, we didn't want to stop. We arrived in Cambodia from the mysterious Myanmar on a plane that I still struggle to understand how it landed; we fell asleep in a tent in the forest of Siem Reap, looking at the lights of the temples of Angkor from above.

We got lost in the streets of Tijuana, where Mars risked his life wearing a turquoise sequin shirt in the city's infamous ghettos, and got lost again in Istanbul's Ammans, where Mars fell in love with all the young Turkish men.

We were invincible, inseparable and happy.

I remember one evening under the stars of the atlas in Morocco, I remember that I said to Mars: "I promise you, maybe not today or tomorrow, but sooner or later we'll find our place in the world, and then we'll build a place that is so beautiful that the whole world will envy us! I'd like it to be a magical place, one that contains everything we've loved... "

Finally, in that very moment, the dream was coming true: we were ready to go.

We had explored many alternatives before getting to the place that we would later decide would become our new home: we thought about Myanmar, a wonderful country, but one whose stability was too precarious to consider living there; then Cambodia, but the reminiscences of a ferocious war still hurt too much and, although the country was wonderful, the hordes of Chinese raping Angkor Wat made me think that everything would soon change quickly, as had already happened in Vietnam.

Then, there was the wild nature of Laos, which left no room for concrete, feasible projects, despite the undisputed beauty of Luang Prabang and the Mekong. Thailand's excesses had already transformed it into an open-air amusement park. Then came Bali, where I had lived for years and, although I adored it, it had lost the charm I had found years earlier.

I was afraid it was a bit late to build something truly unique and we were also looking for somewhere that was still a little unknown to tourism.

Lastly, there was India... of course, its allure had left its mark on us, but investing in that sub-continent and working with Indians scared me a little after the stories I had heard from those who had already done so.

I was sure that what I looked for in Sri Lanka, the "little tear of India", was something that I had never had: a special place that made me feel at home, in a country that was still immature and had infinite potential.

After gaining independence in 1948, Sri Lanka became one of the main liberal democracies in Asia and the game being played on the island was a microcosm of the greater problems in today's world, which is why it fascinated me. Sri Lanka has turned the page: isolated from the world for years, it is now considered one of the twenty most beautiful countries on the planet.

I don't know why, but something in me changed as soon as I set foot on this little island. I had read something before leaving, listlessly leafing through the history of war years that had been forgotten by the world like so many others, stories of a tsunami that was devastating like no other, stories of humble people who were reinventing themselves, whom I had encountered more often in the kitchens of the "fashionable" parts of Milan. After all, Ceylon meant reminiscences: a name that evoked a colonial past and merchants of spices and precious stones.

At the time, I didn't know much more.

It was mid-April when Mars and I first set foot in Colombo; the weather is still mild in that period, the sea is placid, the vegetation is luxuriant, the damp seeps into your bones... but, on the other hand, how many times had I thought about traveling to the tropics "How can a country be so green unless there's at least 100% humidity?".

Mars and I had spoken countless times about crowning our careers as architects by planning and designing a small resort in an Asian country, all on our own.

From the foundations upwards, in fact.

Identifying the right location became obvious, and almost too easy, the moment we arrived in Galle: a town on the south coast (Down South, as they say in these parts). Galle Fort, to be exact.

I had seen plenty of colonial cities in my travels, but this small southern town had something different: a Dutch jewel set in the walls that had saved it from the violence of a terrifying tsunami. However, what made this ancient jewel so wonderful was that the streets were teeming with people who lived, worked and mingled with the few enterprising tourists.

It had been a long time since I had seen such a blue sky; the air felt thin and the rays of the setting sun penetrated the narrow streets of Galle with a surreal light. The city is a succession of dusty streets that still possess all their charm, buildings with white colonnades shaded by immense Mara trees, a tree that only grows here, a few white churches and small fish markets where the tuna glisten in the sun.

Wealthy foreigners have renovated the finest Dutch residences and all manner of boutiques have led to this place deservedly being called the "Saint-Tropez of Sri Lanka". An ancient charm that the Dutch preserve to this day, taking on the maintenance costs and including it in one of the heritage sites protected by UNESCO.

As soon as we arrived in Galle, we stopped for a rest in the main square which, at that hour, was crowded with people queuing as if they were at an English bus stop, waiting to speak with their lawyers or waiting to go and sit in the judge's office: the offices still have handwritten records, like the ones my great grandfather kept for accounting purposes for silk production. No computers, no terminals, no e-mails… fascinating, of course, but only later would that bucolic side of things turn out to be a problem. In the previous days in Colombo, exhausted by the torrid heat of the metropolis, we had contacted almost all the real estate agencies without success. However, they had given me the contact details of a very influential person who managed all the sales of the land in the area, a certain Don Shane, an unlikely surname. Many people here still use the term "Don" before the name, a custom inherited from the Portuguese; indeed, here the Portuguese had preceded the Spaniards, Dutch and English in a succession of dominations that had amputated the dignity of this small corner of the world.

We were exhausted from the journey and the humidity, so we stopped at a small hotel with a decadent charm, large wooden rooms and large four-poster beds. On the veranda of the old hotel, a few distinguished English ladies sipped tea in the cool air produced by large wooden fans.

The following day we were ready to embark upon our search. We had started our adventure by scouring the surroundings and travelling along the old coastal road next to rice fields and golden beaches; I had a keen love for colonial houses that I had seen in magazines, but the colonial houses in Galle often have very small plots, which would be of no use to us, since they belonged to the guardians of neighbouring plantations that had often already been sold.

It took three or four days to see everything, or *nothing*, more accurately speaking. Small dilapidated houses, uncultivated land where only a few cows grazed quietly, abandoned rice fields and large expanses of coconut palms that sold for very little: no one wanted to cultivate them anymore and selling them to foreigners was the only way out sometimes. They left the houses they had lived in for generations and moved into small concrete cubes where, nevertheless, they could afford something more: a gas stove instead of a fire, a mattress and sometimes perhaps even a television.

Other plots were devoid of charm and often situated along impassable roads or patches of beach which had already been built upon too much for my taste. Others were much too far from anywhere. There was nothing that could possibly be compared to what we had in mind.

We had spent seven days wandering the length and breadth of the coast that stretched from Galle to Matara, another charming city on the south coast, and even though the prices were undoubtedly attractive, we still hadn't found anything that had "struck a chord", as we often used to say; we had wandered around every nook in the city to try and savour every smell, every view, every little detail... but time passed quickly and the days are really short in a country straddling the equator, where the sun sets at six o'clock.

Time had flown by and we knew that it wouldn't be an easy task.

Mars would soon be returning to Italy, because he had spent too much time away from his dogs and his latest project; like him, I also had my return ticket, but I don't know why I never got on that plane.

I didn't want to go back to the world I had left so soon. Maybe I needed to be alone for a while, so that's what I did. Mars had pleaded with me to be careful: a young, lonely, white woman alone in a country where foreigners are still considered walking dollar signs and where tourism isn't such a common occurrence could run into trouble. He told me that he would return soon and, in the meantime, I could take things a little easy and settle in.

I reassured him, since I had been through a lot and I was certainly not afraid of new experiences. I was used to travelling alone and, above all, looking after myself. I accompanied him to the train for Colombo, at the old train station that in Galle that looked like a nineteenth-century postcard. As he was leaving, I saw him smile as only he knew how; watching him go off into the distance in those old turquoise carriages, a piece of what I called home was also leaving, the last piece on a long journey of escape.

CHAPTER 2

I had found a quiet place just outside the fort, an old Dutch house in a very quiet area with a small garden and a cool patio; I decided to stop thinking about land, perches and hectares for a few days, I just wanted to relax and enjoy the scent of that new world.

I had met a nice old man who proudly used his tuk-tuk to take me wherever I asked him to go, following me everywhere I went, even when we walked through the dusty streets of the city. We never talked. He would fall silent immediately after running out of the only words he knew in English: "Mam, where are you from?" and "How long you stay?".

The rest was a succession of good-natured smiles and small movements of the head, as I was only was used to seeing here and in India. I had met some nice people who lived near the small house and had started communicating with them as best we could.

I managed to understand that the Sinhalese didn't like talking about the tsunami or the war, memories that were still too raw and hadn't been erased. Or the British: they didn't hate them, but claimed that they had stolen almost a hundred years of their culture and were responsible for what had happened in the fierce war against the Tamil ethnic group. Conversations were simple and concise, while their smiles and kindness stopped me from feeling too intrusive.

I often ate alone in the small restaurants and stalls in the city: very spicy *roti* or succulent *rice and curry*, under the curious gazes of the men and the suspicious ones of the women; a foreign woman, alone... they thought "why", "is she not married?", "where is her husband?".

I couldn't tell my story, it was still too painful. They had been tranquil days and that's the way I wanted them to stay. I walked tirelessly until the evening and beyond, when the women picked fragrant jasmine flowers to take to the temple, flowers that only emit their scent at that time of night, as if knowing they were ready to be picked; I walked peacefully even when the lights of the houses were turned on and shortly afterwards went out.

At 9 pm everything would stop, it was already late at night.

The days were marked by waking up with the bread cart playing unlikely music by Beethoven, which ended up getting into your head until it went away and you still seemed to hear it. They continued with the children who went to school in their immaculate uniforms, which made them all look the same: no rich, poor, well-to-do or beggars; small, tidy, toy soldiers, happy to find a little joy outside the walls of their small houses in the middle of nowhere.

The women had already prepared the *rice and curry* for the afternoon and dinner, while the men had already left for their modest jobs or were busy working in the fields.

I would go around for hours in my personal tuk-tuk, covering a handful of miles, which seemed endless; we stopped to visit small white temples and immaculate, golden beaches. I spent every morning on the seafront in Galle, where engaged couples embraced under the umbrellas that protected their intimacy, made up of small gestures. There were dozens of them every morning, all lined up, and they promised each other eternal love. Sinhalese are still very chaste and closely bound to their traditions: young couples are often "promised by their families", so these normally clandestine little love stories had to take place in secret.

Among the others I had met during that period, I had also met Nirosh, who worked in a nice hotel in the town centre: a meek man who spoke excellent English and who immediately came across as very open and friendly. His calm and kind manner struck me right away... we often talked when I went for a drink in that nice hotel. He told me about the fort, about how it had been fortunate to survive and that he had always lived there with his family. He told me his story, which was much like that of many others.

He told me about when he had met his young wife and that, not having the financial means to get married, they had remained engaged for 11 years without practically touching each other, since tradition, which is still very much in use, states that women must be virgins until their wedding day. He told me that he had respected her all that time because, if by chance he had died, she would never have been able to marry anyone else. A great gesture of love that this meek man continued to express for his family every single day.

He told me that, thanks to his salary, he had managed to stop his wife from having to cook three times a day, as is the norm here, but sometimes go out to eat. He was very proud of what he was able to do for his family and I asked him to tell me more.

He explained that the situation of women in Sri Lanka, despite being the first country in Asia with a female prime minister, is still very precarious. Young women often marry by proxy and accept their fate with a smile, especially in central and northern villages, where they are promised to men who are unknown to their family.

The lives of the Sinhalese are marked by precise events: birth, often at home, and immediately afterwards a horoscope is created that follows the person for their entire life and will decide their luck, happiness, fertility and end.

Young girls are celebrated when they reach puberty by the whole extended family in a ceremony that lasts seven days, locked in a room and only let out when their menstruation is over; as was also the case for us in towns down south, young brides have to display their scarlet sheet to the village after the wedding night... otherwise they can be repudiated!

They often only marry for the community, they always have children because in their culture it is unthinkable not to continue the circle of life and, in any case, children guarantee future sustenance; they age early, die and, even then, their bodies are displayed to members of the community, often by the roadside. Indeed, I remembered that one day I happened to walk through the streets of Unawatuna, the most popular beach in the south, and in the midst of tourists in shorts and Chinese people with parasols, I saw the body of a recently deceased man displayed in a shop window, as if he were merchandise, a few yards from the main road.

So, a life (and a death) spent on display, accepting the rules of a rigorous culture.

There are realities that are very distant from what we would like, especially in an era in which women live in constant search for stability and a sense of recognition in the society that surrounds them. In Sri Lanka, the female figure is still fragile today and continually a victim of abuse, not only by torturers, but above all due to laws that do not yet provide true protection.

During the civil war, which saw these areas subjected not only to massacres, but also to rapes and kidnappings, especially involving minors, many women were abused: as often happens in wars.

In Sri Lanka, a woman becomes a victim of sexual violence every 90 seconds, even now. However, the abuse of women does not stop at rape: they are often exploited and poorly paid at the workplace; most of the time, they find themselves forced to go abroad to look for a job so that they can support their families.

He told me that Sri Lankan female workers pay the highest price to dress the world.

They churn out clothes that are sold throughout Europe and the United States, often for well-known brands. The workforce, sometimes from the remotest countryside, is often made up of very young women who come from places that are more than a hundred miles away. These female workers toil for twelve to fourteen hours a day, without breaks.

Along the road to the village, I often saw leaflets stuck to lampposts: companies recruit using photos of women with broad smiles and a large printed figure. "You can earn up to twenty-four thousand rupees a month"... which is around 150 euros a month.

Sri Lanka's patriarchal society, which is so ingrained in its history, is also intensely perpetuated by the use of marriage as a social institution. Although women may work in parallel with most household chores, they are still marginalised because it is deemed socially improper to venture outside the domestic sphere!

One of the plagues still afflicting Sri Lanka is early marriage, which is the phenomenon of unions at an early age, which are of great concern, especially when thinking of the devastating psychological and physical repercussions that it entails. Young victims, not yet mature enough to face the experiences of adulthood, marriage and motherhood, face considerable risks. "Child brides" are particularly prone to complications during pregnancy and childbirth, as well as running a high risk of contracting the HIV virus. Furthermore, they often fall victim to domestic violence and abuse.

The determining factors driving this practice are poverty, religious dictates and the belief that marriage strengthens the prestige and honour of a family.

Speaking with a dozen girls from the neighbouring village, I found that five of them had never used sanitary towels. They use old cloths. Lack of access to sanitary towels not only leads girls to skip school for fear of getting blood stains on their clothes and other related inconveniences, it is also a danger to their health. Using cloths and rags instead of sanitary towels can cause infections, as well as serious conditions such as cervical cancer, which is the second most common cancer among Sri Lankan women.

In short, instead of equating the conditions of women to those of men, they once again proved exactly how closed minded it's possible to be towards the female gender, even now.

In short, Sri Lankan politics, institutions and laws were a real disaster, but I still had respect for this proud people and their strength, as well as their determination to accept whatever was imposed upon them.

Everything I saw helped me a lot to understand how to try and relate to them.

I began to understand why the men looked at me that way; who knows what they might have thought of an enterprising European woman who had gone there to build a hotel, when their women spent their lives sacrificing them for theirs.

I realised that it would be really hard for me to maintain the role that I would have to play over the following months, managing a building site where only men worked.

Being a woman, guide and manager of other people in a world of men, in which that role was reserved exclusively to the male gender. Still, I had to try and, with Mars' help, it would be possible.

CHAPTER 3

Before having to deal with the problem of assuming the right role and making people respect me, I still needed to look for the right place to start my work. I hadn't heard any news about land from Don Shane and had almost lost hope of finding anything that might even come close to what I wanted.

Then, one morning, he called me early to tell me that we had forgotten to see one last plot of land in Boussa, a small town near Galle, along the ancient road that leads back to Colombo.

I was a bit disappointed, but I decided to go anyway.

We went a few miles up the coast, then I saw a detour with a small sign, "Water for elephant". Not a bad start!

We travelled another five hundred yards inland and I saw a small road that took the same route as the oldest railway in the country, some dignified houses and then a narrow path that climbed towards the jungle. And then, there it was: surrounded by cinnamon plantations and wind-tilted palm trees, along the bend of the river, lay an expanse of deep green grass dotted with slender coconut palms and a small farmhouse with an ancient soul.

It's impossible to explain what happens inside when you find the right place!

There's no special reason, I think it's just how you feel, and I felt at home. I was speechless. It was almost five o'clock in the afternoon, the most beautiful and poetic time of day: a myriad of white herons frolicked in the blinding green grass and a family of peacocks seemed to be at home there; a few undisturbed cows grazed and the scent of cinnamon intoxicated the air. A strange feeling came over me immediately and I couldn't hide my enthusiasm, I didn't want to leave that place, ever.

I asked Don Shane to be alone for a moment, I wanted to enjoy all this in private.

I got the keys from him and said that I would bring them to him the following day. Without making a fuss, he turned the big black car around and drove away.

It was 1 May 2014 when I entered the gate of Wirdana.

It was almost dark, thousands of fireflies shone in that darkness, it was enchanting, I had never seen so many in my life, they seemed to light up on my order to show me the way, I walked in that shimmering light and it was like I was dreaming, I would have wanted to stay there forever, but it was too late. I would be going back the next morning. I walked back along the dusty street with a strange smile stamped on my face; I smiled at passers-by and felt like shouting to the entire world: I've found it, that's it!

I couldn't sleep that night.

I woke up early and, even though it was still night-time at home, I called Mars and told him about this fantastic place that I thought was perfect for our project because it had everything we needed.

"If you think it's special, it's special for me, too...", he said, and I knew him so well that I knew he meant it.

I wanted to go back there immediately, without wasting time. The tuk-tuk left me a bit far from the exact place this time, so I passed a small, old station and an old Buddhist temple where the lights of the puja still sparkled and someone had started the day praying.

I loved that time of day, when the world awakens; there was no noise and the light was wonderful. I entered through the ramshackle gate, sat near the portico of the colonial house for a moment as if wanting to savour the atmosphere before entering. It was early, perhaps seven o'clock, but it was already hot.

I had learnt that if I stayed silent and closed my eyes, then the voice of nature would become clearer and clearer: first there was nothing, then the singing of birds, then the wind, and I slowly began to hear the distant sound of a Mantra coming from the nearby temple... I closed my eyes again and the chant of the Muezzin on the opposite side began to overlap the litany: how was that possible?

I also heard the bell of a church in the distance; everything merged into a single mystical sound: I took it as a sign: my place could be here and here alone.

I had the keys, so I entered the front door; I had to bow my head so that I could go through. Inside, a magical light filtered through the old ceiling beams. In the kitchen there was still a wok burnt on the ashes and lots of glass flasks in small crevices on the mouldy wall. The smell was that of vegetable concoctions that were reminiscent of the oils used in Ayurveda in India.

The wall of one room was covered with improbable writings that looked like lace, some numbers and formulas that I was unable to understand; there were also writings in English and drawings of small plants and leaves lined up.

I went out the back, there were fruit plants and others that I had never seen before everywhere, exotic flowers and cinnamon barks that gave off a special scent. I walked to the edge of the property: the path led straight to a small rice field where lotus flowers had taken the place of rice. Below me, there were the signs of the passage of someone who, for years, probably every morning, had walked down that path.

I almost felt like I was being followed, but in a good way. As if I were being accompanied by a silent guardian. From that distant perspective, I abandoned the romanticism for a moment and returned to my role as an architect so that I could imagine how everything might look. After making a mental sketch of what I would have liked to see, everything turned out to be as perfect as I had imagined.

I was meant to give Don Shane an answer that very evening, but I didn't wait for night to fall before calling him and unconditionally accepting his proposal: it was a done deal!

Well, more or less. The procedures for the sale of land, as they are back home, require you to examine the documents relating to the last owners to assess whether there are any outstanding mortgages or other matters; this involved going to the offices in Galle, a kind of circle of hell where a myriad of people waited in line for their turn. Over the following days, I also joined the queue, in that place that I had only seen from afar on the days following my arrival. It was a good feeling to mix with them and become invisible for a day, but unfortunately you are never transparent here and I would soon realise as much. Indeed, they already knew everything about me at the office, they had already prepared all the rigorously handwritten files and only handed me the deed of sale with a date on the cover after hours of waiting:

1 May 1958, Nande Wijesinghe

At the time, I didn't notice the coincidence of the dates and the name on the documents, it was hot and I was in a hurry to finish up. It all seemed right, as right as things can be in a country where not all the population is registered yet, but I soon learned that I shouldn't ask too many questions because there weren't any answers and, if I wanted to make progress, despite my misgivings I had to trust people who often have to live on lies in order to survive.

Shane joined me shortly thereafter and made me sign some papers; the officer put a stamp on the old land registry map, while a young woman wrote something in a file by hand. There were thousands of binders and land registry maps from every era and I thought that perhaps some of the land still dated back to the time of the settlers.

A pre-war fan creaked above us and blew the old documents around, raising dust that had collected over decades and everything seemed ancient in the backlight; it was a detail that I cannot forget.

A quick handshake between the employees and Shane and that was that: the deal was signed and I had managed to negotiate to pay for the land in instalments over the months that followed.

CHAPTER 4

I decided to move house and rent a small room overlooking the sea a few yards from my land.

The house was owned by an Italian lady from Naples called Caterina who was kind to me, but still not very integrated with the locals even after a number of years, having never really tried.

It was a simple, yet convenient place from which to walk to Wirdana and there was a beautiful, tourist-free beach with golden sand where there was just a group of houses that belonged to fishermen who would head out every night left on rickety outriggers and return in the morning loaded with lobsters and tuna which they traded for a pack of cigarettes, which are a luxury here and are still sold individually. The beach was covered in seeds that I had never seen before, jewels that were carved and carried by the waves from who knows where, which sprout as soon as they touch the ground, giving give life to other plants that join those already there to form a shade of green the intensity of which I had never seen.

I often liked to take walks at sunset, which in those months was beautiful, with the climate perfect for my long strolls and the light wonderful.

I often stopped at a small hut preceded by a white flag inviting people to Baradise Beach. I was fascinated by how the local boys had transformed the place into a beautiful corner of the beach.

Bara was a boy with dreadlocks, after whom the beach took its amusing name. He had bright, astute eyes.

He had turned the place into a kind of Puerto Escondido and made the best Mojito I had ever drunk. The music was great. There weren't many places like it, with its improvised style; there was a transgressive, yet alluring atmosphere. That place had become a reference point for me. We immediately struck up a special understanding and the fact that I would soon be building something just a stone's throw from there had created a sort of tacit complicity with those guys.

I often went there to draw and the concept of Wirdana took form with each passing day. My project had to be the concentrate of everything I had seen and appreciated during my travels around the globe. I began to imagine what it would be like.

The courtyard of the old house had inspired me to design an ancient central area in the middle of the building, where cool air would enter during the day and turn into a light breeze in the evening, serving to ventilate the entire building as is customary in countries that subjected to the humid heat of the tropics.

It had to be a place of calm and peace where serenity would reign, somewhere to meditate at dawn and end the day with a relaxing Ayurvedic massage. A large swimming pool reflecting the colour of nature and a place to fresh up with some special food, perhaps even a few recipes from the past. The products needed were available in abundance.

The nearby market would provide fresh vegetables with unusual names and delicious fruit every day. The fish caught each morning came from a sea overflowing with so much prey that the nets were unable hold it all; sometimes, the fish shone so much in the sun that it felt like walking into a jewellery store. I imagined European ladies tasting the delicacies from the garden or the mangoes from my trees.

And then, of course, the guest villas: there shouldn't be many of them, perhaps six, built in my style, but with local details and materials. An outdoor bathroom was a must in order to enjoy a shower under the shade of a frangipani. I kept thinking that if I wanted to keep something of that old house, I couldn't destroy it, even if it was too small to just be renovated... yet I felt that preserving something was a duty to those who had loved that place, cultivated those plants, walked the paths every morning and maybe, who knows, ended their days there. I thought I could keep the old windows that could be converted into coffee tables or perhaps a decoration in the massage room. Perhaps I might keep the old tiles that could be used on my portico. Maybe a few colonial decorations to embellish the rooms.

That day, I left my mojito half-finished and went back to Wirdana, because I couldn't wait to go back to see those old windows and figure out what could be salvaged, also because demolition would soon begin.

It was almost dark when I arrived at Wirdana, the light at that time of day was magical as always, mixing with that of the sunset and making everything shine: the palms turn silver and everything seems part of an old black and white film. There was only the sound of birds and the magic of the fireflies made me think of what that place would be like in the evening, in the light of torches, the last rays of the sun filtering through the windows and the colonial friezes.

I went to a window made from teak, a precious wood that even the poorest here used; there was only an old bed made of rope and some terracotta bowls in the room. I tried to open the window, but something was blocking it: I pushed a little harder and realised that an old notebook was stuck between the wooden friezes. It was dark now and I could only make out one thing on the cover: "Nande, 1 May 1943".

I decided to take it, even though it felt like I was stealing it from someone. I hurried back to my shelter by the sea with my ill-gotten gains, like a thief. I had a canopied bed with a mosquito net which I closed quickly, like a child who had stolen some sweets, so that I could hide from the world and devote myself to some reading.

I took a closer look at the little treasure: it was an old notebook containing botanical drawings and explanations of tea plants, formulas of indecipherable mixtures, as well as thoughts written in English. "We weighed 150 pounds today, the owner is happy with me".

I quickly leafed through the notebook, as if someone was spying on me, as if I was doing something wrong.

I was only spying on the life of another person who lived in that place for goodness knows how many years and, who knows, perhaps ended their days there.

Simple thoughts about someone who must have worked on a plantation. Other signs seemed to mark the passage of time and the notebook also contained some faded photographs, some handwritten receipts for money and some recipes, all written in English.

Lastly, I found a letter that had worn with age, as if it had been read a thousand times.

I wondered how many mysteries were in that little notebook!

CHAPTER 5

Mars would be back the next day, looking forward to seeing what I had done.

It would be nice to have a piece of home there with me again, I couldn't wait to tell him everything that had happened to me, as excited as a child.

It had been too long and by then I had already found our builder with Caterina's help. He was a guy from Hikkaduwa named Sam: he had only been in the business a short while, but he knew a lot. I was told that he had been a coral collector, a fisherman, then a labourer and, after the tsunami, he had built a small non-profit project for an Austrian company, but above all they told me that he knew everything about the area: perhaps he also knew something about that Nande person and his notebook, I thought.

Over the phone, I arranged to meet at the property that morning. I'm usually on time, indeed, I'm often early, but that day I stopped at the temple to feed some puppies and when I arrived he was already there. I had always appreciated the looks of Indian men and the best-looking ones are probably better than any other ethnicity; I had seen many on my travels, but when I saw Sam I was blinded by his smile.

"Hi, madam!"

He was tall and the colour of his skin was like the ebony of the chairs on display on the stalls of the antique dealers in Galle. I couldn't speak much; I swallowed, then tried to focus so I could explain what I wanted in a few words and I realised while I was speaking that he was also able to read between the lines of my enthusiastic, excited explanations. We visited the entire property, sharing the thoughts and emotions of that magical place.

I refrained from immediately talking to him about the man in the old house, even if I would have wanted to, since too many people had told me that talking a lot would be like demonstrating an inappropriate amount of familiarity. Instead, I decided to listen. It was he who spoke and, shortly afterwards, he told me about the tsunami and that he had been saved only because he was fishing offshore when it struck; he told me about the devastating wave that had swept away his village in a few seconds, about how he had rescued children and old people clinging to palm trees to save themselves, about how members of their families had been declared missing for days, about the devastating smell of corpses and of fishing boats found miles away.

The huts in his village had literally been swept away by the fury of the waves. The inhabitants stood in front of what had been their homes, dazed. Unable to move a finger, paralysed by sorrow and despair, they weren't even able to clean the mud off the few objects that had escaped the fury of the sea: they were inert, resigned. People didn't have the strength to get back onto their own two feet and were waiting for help.

He told me that Galle was a cross between a giant traffic jam and a frightening biblical exodus. Hundreds of men in vehicles and on bicycles wandering around as if nothing had happened among the corpses of women and children that had been handed back by the water or buried under piles of rubble and mud. What had been one of the pearls of southern Sri Lanka until the day before had become a pile of rubble, from which emanated the smell of naphtha mixed with that of decaying bodies.

There was no longer a building standing on Galle's seafront: the sea had taken the street vendors' kiosks and the shops on the beach first, gutting them. Then it went further, raging against houses and shacks. The only things left were bricks, mud, remains of walls, rags of a thousand colours, fragments of doors and windows and goods from the shops.

The bus station, behind the central square and about two hundred yards from the beach, had been struck hard by the tsunami. Buses had been thrown on top of cars, which had been thrown on top of other buses, forming a jumbled mass of metal sheets a hundred yards away from the point where the wave had struck the vehicles.

The inferno was same in Unawatuna, three and a half miles east of Galle, or Hikkaduwa. What had been Galle's fleet of fishing boats had been piled up high on the waterfront by the wave, an intertwining mass of nets and colours.

In fact, the whole South coast had become a deathly stage. You just needed to move closer to the sea to realise it, he had told me: it was surreal; up to a mile from the coast, it was as if nothing had happened; then all hell began. The corpses remained in the streets by the dozen, sometimes covered haphazardly, sometimes not even that. Many were children, their little hands sticking out of the rags that someone had thrown on top of them.

People looked and walked straight by. There was not even the slightest attempt to organise an emergency service and it was impossible to calculate the number of dead, which was undoubtedly several thousand.

The police, army, navy and air force limited their efforts to monitoring the situation with ships, helicopters and soldiers. Although no one knows exactly what they were monitoring. Those who had survived like he had done, however, seemed to accept what had happened to them as if it had been fate, trying to smile and get on with their lives despite the dead lying in the streets.

One and a half miles from Hikkaduwa, a few miles from his house, a train had derailed. There were between five hundred and a thousand people on board: no one would ever know the exact number. They were still there, buried in that iron box. He said that the bodies that the sea had handed back looked like dolls, swollen and unrecognisable. In Galle, they had moved them to the lawn in the square on the seafront, so that anyone recognising them could prepare a coffin and a funeral.

I was shivering because I felt like I was there. The places were the same and even now many houses had remained petrified, just as they were on the day of the tsunami: ruins that remained there as a reminder. He told me that international aid had arrived quickly, but unfortunately it also brought many problems with it.

Given one of the administrations with the highest rate of corruption in the world, the undertaking had immediately proved difficult, with the aggravating circumstance of a civil war between the Tamil minority and the Sinhalese majority which, instead of subsiding, had become invigorated, further fuelled by accusations regarding the poor distribution of funds for the victims.

If the aid figures released by the coordinating bodies were true, the funds raised would have been three times more than needed by the population. However, many international NGOs complained that it was impossible to monitor the proper distribution of aid, under pressure - according to numerous testimonies - from local politicians and state officials. According to one of these reports, as many as fifteen thousand families in the north-western part of the country, which had not even been touched by the cataclysm, have inappropriately received monthly subsistence allowances.

Due to these and other reasons, most of the people affected by the disaster, who didn't have their own homes or land, were still living in temporary housing. Post-tsunami reconstruction was used to promote the "big business" of tourism in the country, regardless of the needs of the people affected by the disaster.

Poor communities were removed from the coasts of Sri Lanka to make room for large hotel complexes. Immediately after the tsunami, the country's government announced that the population would not be able to rebuild their homes along the coast, but those measures were not designed to protect the fishing communities.

"The government wasn't trying to protect them, it was forcing them to make room for tourism", he told me.

It was all true: along the whole of the southern coast, which had been struck by the wave, huge hotel complexes had been erected which, in addition to disfiguring the coast, had no reason to exist and were clearly overestimated. They had undoubtedly become piggy banks for corrupt politicians.

I understood why many locals had started to found small non-profit organisations with the help of private sponsors, so as to directly help their families and their villages.

He also showed me the scars on his legs, scars that the debris had caused as he was trying to save himself by swimming underwater. I listened without uttering a single word.

He had a son, who had been born when he was very young, and a child bride who had left years earlier, fleeing from a marriage that had been arranged by her mother. He was left on his own to take care of his son, his various jobs and a small house where he lived with his old parents.

He had a sad look, even though his smile was bright and disarming at the same time. I didn't notice how fast time had gone by; we had gone all around the property, talked about the project and much more. His enthusiasm filled me with excitement.

We would soon begin construction.

I was happy and couldn't wait to start, we walked to the beach together. He brushed me as we walked and I felt a shiver.

So, I could still feel something… some of my senses were still alive and they hadn't all died along with my memories. The pain had not killed everything in me, I could still feel alive, let feelings of pleasure, attraction and complicity flow through me.

Sam and I chatted so much that we were very late to the appointment with Mars, who in the meantime had arrived from Italy. When he saw me with him, he made a strange expression with his face: as always, he had already understood. I got rid of Sam quickly, almost feeling guilty for something I hadn't done, and coldly told him we would see each other the next day.

I already knew what Mars was going to say.

We didn't talk much that evening and I avoided looking him in the eye, since we knew each other too well to lie. He was tired from the trip, so I told him to rest and that we would talk the following day.

I didn't sleep very well that night. I don't know if it was the thought of Sam, the excitement for the new project or the heat that made the air humid and unbearable. I went out on the veranda to get some air; I was too agitated.

I sat in the open air and looked at the sky, losing myself as I gazed into night, at the stars and into distant space, in which our planet appeared small and insignificant in the vastness of the universe.

I needed to feel alive and get away from myself and what I was doing would help me get through the pain for a few minutes. I had died too many times over the past two years.

I died with him in a hospital room.

However, the time had come to let him go and be reborn: that's what he would have wanted, I was certain. There, away from all prejudices, it seemed so easy! I didn't owe an explanation to anyone, I was slowly taking back my life and I could deal whatever came next.

I smiled, remembering my love one last time that evening. The pain was there and would remain, but there were also all the good things we had experienced together.

My heart began to beat again. It wasn't healed, but it was alive. That's the way I wanted it to stay.

CHAPTER 6

The days that followed were hectic: Mars and I had to make up for lost time; I had to show him everything I had seen and quickly convey my enthusiasm to him. I told him about the notebook and about Nande, about the feeling I had every time I went to Wirdana, as if someone were following me, about how I had integrated into the country and, for the first time, I saw he was a little surprised.

When he left for Italy after a few weeks, I had a strange feeling. For the first time, I felt that that world, so different and often difficult to understand, was not for everyone. Not everyone was able to appreciate the little nuances that I found myself noticing... maybe time had changed Mars a bit, maybe we weren't ready at the same time. In any event, he promised that he would be back soon.

Meanwhile, as the days went by, I saw Sam more and more often. Our conversations were becoming more intimate, our minds closer and our thoughts increasingly on the same wavelength. We spent the evenings planning together, we dreamed of what it would be like. He often went away for hours and I worked while waiting for him to return.

At that point everything was ready to begin, but he explained to me that before starting any construction work it was necessary to have an auspicious ceremony focussed on removing any negativity and giving the location all the benevolence of the gods, whichever they may be.

That day he told me to join him at nine o'clock in the evening.

I arrived early and it seemed like a dream: they had lit hundreds of small oil lamps and large banana leaf lamps along the edges of Wirdana. It was beautiful, they looked like fireflies or even stars. The crickets and cicadas sang, as is typical on summer nights.

They were waiting for me before putting an aromatic oil provided by the monk of the temple, considered a good omen, into a hole in the ground: the first brick would then be laid there; I had to cover it with earth and pray for a few minutes while the lights went out one by one. It was a fantastic evening.

We sat in a circle and they began to sing; my dream would come true in that place and then there was *him* by my side, watching from above. Now everything seemed easier and more at hand. I was happy to have experienced that magical moment: who knows if Nande had done the same when he had built the small house and marked the boundary of the plantation!

That night I resumed reading the notebook I had left aside for a few days and I realised that certain pages showed the signs of those who count the days one after the other, as if waiting for something. The signs marked time without revealing any sign of anonymous, particular events or occurrences.

Nande was undoubtedly a botanist, but that wasn't difficult to figure out due to the amount of plants and herbs that filled the garden. The pages of the notebook were all mixed up and I was unable to put them into chronological order, except for a few dates marked here and there.

The recipes also mentioned miraculous plants that healed all kinds of diseases and precious ointments that healed the skin; it was strange, partly because the man who had written the notebook spoke excellent English, but every now and then wrote in his native language, as if he sometimes conversing with someone who didn't understand him.

I would soon ask someone about Nande, because his story, simple as it was, was a mystery to me.

I put my notebook down and went to sleep, also because we were going to start work the next day. I had given precise instructions on how to preserve all the old tiles, the windows and identify the centre of the inner courtyard, which would remain as it was; the centrepiece of my project. A small bulldozer was all that was needed to demolish what remained of those old paper walls; the house fell in on itself, but its outline clearly marked the area for excavation. I felt a strong sense of sadness: how could I do this to Nande?

I promised myself that I would respect his work, continue to care for his plants and learn his secrets. I knew only too well what it meant to erase something, but I also knew that material things come and go... and yet, the memory of what we do stays in the hearts of those who are left forever.

Sam and I worked hard and spent the time together, but every now and then he disappeared without giving an explanation. I didn't want to ask too much, but the time I spent with him was nevertheless peaceful and I liked the way he always understood what I had in mind without my having to explain anything; a thin thread bound us tightly and I began to feel really close to him.

One day, he didn't show up; it was pouring down with rain and I waited for him for hours, but there wasn't even a phone call or a message. He often disappeared for days for no reason and then reappeared without providing any explanation. The next day, I showed up at the construction site and said nothing, hoping that he would speak, but that's the way things are here, if you don't ask a specific question no one will tell you anything, and if it is not a really precise question, you'll receive an evasive answer or a lie.

We didn't talk all day, we had a lot to do. We stayed late to work that evening. However, I noticed a sadness in his eyes and at one point he hugged me as he had never done before. I reciprocated in silence, without asking him for an explanation, because I understood that he didn't need or want to talk, he only wanted to have someone close.

He arrived early the following morning, there was an odd expression on his face and his black eyes were wide open. He looked at the phone and seemed to be waiting for someone or something. At that point, I was worried and drew close.

"What's going on, Sam?"

As usual, he failed to answer. After a while, a black car arrived and stopped at the end of the road. I saw him go to the car and two men got out, talking loudly.

Sam shook his head several times: it was a yes, but it looked like a no, it was a yes, but only later did I realise that it was meant as a no: now I know! The two men left after a while and he came back and sat next to me. I had understood that there was something terrible in his eyes. He hugged me again, then showed me his phone: it was a family photo, I recognised him, his son, an old woman and an elderly European lady wearing a strange expression on her face.

I didn't understand what he wanted to tell me.

He showed me another photo, him and the elderly lady standing in front of what looked like a school; then another in which there was him, that same woman and ten other people and another which also included the two men who I'd seen getting out of the car.

My head was spinning, I didn't understand.

He looked at me for a moment and just said: "My family is more important than my happiness".

To understand everything properly I would have had to ask some specific questions. Who were the men in the car? What was happening? Eventually, he explained everything, perhaps because my bewildered expression and questioning gaze made him cave in.

Sam's family was helped by an Austrian woman who supported everyone: his son could study thanks to her and a hundred children belonging to a non-profit organisation they had created depended on funding from that same elderly woman, whose name I didn't even know and who did it all in exchange for Sam, who was meant to stay with her and satisfy her "appetites".

I was speechless.

Sam's life was for sale? How could that be?

He told me that his family had decided everything, that the men in the car had followed me for days because they had understood that something could develop between us and I was in the way of their mistress's project.

I would have been in danger. He couldn't put me in such a predicament, because they would also have boycotted the work at Wirdana. He told me about a very influential cousin who had benefited from the Austrian lady's project with enough money to look after the entire village and that someone close to him had attempted to kill him when he had tried to leave her.

I didn't know what to say.

He looked at me, his eyes full of tears; I braced myself and, even though I was dying inside, I merely explained that sometimes we have to sacrifice our happiness for something more important. I also explained that very strong relationships exist even though the people involved are not a couple, that people can be close without touching each other and that certain elective affinities last forever.

We both knew what was going on between us, but we had a lot of work to do, great responsibilities and we couldn't let our feelings take over.

"I will always be behind you", he said. And that would be enough for both of us.

It would be difficult for something similar to occur in our culture, but it was normal for those who need to survive, or at least very common after the advent of tourists, who despite themselves had brought an awareness of how easy it could be to achieve economic stability with them. I soon realised that, unfortunately, this was not the only aspect and that there were also lots of sexual abuses and crimes related to paedophilia and sex tourism; I realised that Sri Lankan youngsters were very fragile and vulnerable.

A large number of youngsters committed suicide, the highest rate in the world after Japan. Sometimes they would throw themselves off a cliff or drink rat poison.

However, that was certainly not the case with us, Sam would continue his work and, thanks to that, one day he might perhaps be free. Indeed, there was still something important we had to do together and we both knew it.

Despite everything, I was no longer able to suffer. I had learned to manage pain and I was able to shake it off like a wet dog shakes off water. All in all, I felt stronger and calmer.

I knew I would succeed yet again.

CHAPTER 7

Despite everything, Wirdana was beginning to take shape: the foundations were already laid and outlined the shape of what would be the new building. The horoscope that we had consulted, as was the custom before embarking upon any kind of activity, had decided that there had to be an odd number of windows, the measurements needed to be changed and the internal divisions modified in part with respect to my initial design.

I was a little angry at first, but I soon realised that I would have to adapt to these beliefs, since I could not go back. So, I accepted the changes. Who knows if Nande had also consulted the horoscope when building the windows that way?

I counted them: there were nine, eight columns in the portico and five layers of tiles, just like Sam said. I didn't object and although usually no one interferes in my work as an architect, this time I understood that I was the one who needed to adapt to them and this would undoubtedly not be the last time.

The weather was slowly changing, the sea was getting blacker and the wind on the beach prevented me from taking my long walks. The rainy season was beginning; not a monsoon like the one in India that appears suddenly and paralyses everything and everyone, but rains that slowly increase in intensity and strike the central regions. The great rivers that descend towards the coast expand like hot air balloons and flood everything in their path, swelling up to form waves of water that submerge everything. Houses, trees, plantations. This was the case with the Gin Ganga River, which also flooded part of my land on the bend of the river. The water submerged roads, things, sometimes entire villages... we suspended the work, since it was raining too much.

One morning, Sam came calling to tell me that we absolutely had to go to the construction site. That day I arrived at Wirdana and I will never forget what appeared before my eyes: everything was submerged, at least three feet of black mud and water had covered everything: the land, foundations, wood, materials... everything had to be pulled out of there as soon as possible in order to salvage at least some of it.

The guys and Sam began working in the deluge; their houses had also been flooded, like everything else, yet they continued working up to their waists in water to save the construction site. They were carrying huge teak beams that absolutely needed to be salvaged.

For my part, I helped as much as I could, organising and helping with the "logistics", if we can call it that. It was strange, I wasn't in a panic, partly because the guys were calm and even though some of them had lost everything, they still ventured to play in the water, splashing each other and laughing like children.

They quickly managed to salvage part of the most important and expensive materials, but most of the work had been destroyed, buried by tons of mud. I couldn't help but think that those people were there, working for me, while they were losing everything they owned.

The surrounding villages had suffered enormous damage and many people had lost their lives; the more fortunate had only lost their houses, yet no one was discouraged. They would rebuild, they said. Once their loved ones had been buried, they would roll up their sleeves and put their modest lives back together; it was a great lesson on life for me.

Flooding that year had been really intense, the whole country had suffered damage and a large section of the population was left with nothing. It hadn't been possible to stem that quantity of water.

What would have happened had the building been finished? That scared me.

In that moment, however, the problem was that months-worth of work had disappeared in an instant. We decided to raise the entire plot, as Nande had done around the small house. We used the same stones and the same height; it was as if I trusted him: who knows how many times he had found himself in similar circumstances!

We followed the same procedures Nande had used for the small house and raised everything more than three feet above ground level. The rain never seemed to stop, the electricity went off every hour and we remained isolated, sometimes unable to communicate with the rest of the world, let alone able to continue work.

The only thing we could do in those moments was wait, because the rain blocked the cars and tractors, while the red mud even managed to seep into our bones. Buses came and went in fits and starts, tuk-tuks skidded in the wet. It was hard to even leave the house, but Nande kept me company.

I took advantage of the bad weather to read the notebook. I learnt about the powers of Neem oil, how to defeat parasites, the name of Ayurvedic medicines, the coconut compound to make plants grow and how to heal small wounds.

Around that time, I got an e-mail from Mars saying he would be coming soon because he had to talk to me. He arrived the following week, his plane landing after negotiating the black clouds on yet another rainy day. We had dinner in a beautiful place by the sea, where turtles usually swim and lay their eggs. It was easy to see them when they emerged with their little heads on their big bodies and sometimes they even let people touch them. There was a thatched roof and we could keep our feet in the water, even though it was still raining heavily.

That evening, Mars told me that big financial problems had arisen and he was afraid he was making a bad investment. So, he said he would help me if I needed it, but he also added that he had to abandon the project. The flood had been the straw that broke the camel's back, but I couldn't force him to stay and I didn't want to waste energy trying to convince him.

I, on the other hand, could not give up and so I suddenly found myself on my own. By then I already knew that other people only accompany us for a period of your life and that, when all is said and done, we are alone to face our destiny. I didn't blame him, although I was undoubtedly sad, but I knew that the project was now mine alone.

Despite everything and everyone, the monsoon came to an end towards July. The sea became calm and the days sunny. By then, Nande had taught me about the seasons of the moon and rice, the months in which mangoes ripen, when coconuts transform their tender hearts into a hard pulp. I knew when the sacred season began, in which pilgrims climb Adams Peak. I had learnt that the wind would change with a full moon and the times when farmers planted and harvested cinnamon.

I had learnt a bit of Sinhala, the language of the Sinhalese, but that strange alphabet, which was halfway between caricatures of stylised pigs and laughing frogs, was so difficult to decipher!

A single letter had twelve declensions and the guttural sounds seemed impossible for me to pronounce. I must have sounded ridiculous when I spoke, because everyone laughed, but to me it felt like a little gesture that brought me closer to them. Even if only a little.

I often went to the nearby temple, a peaceful place carved into the rock; I had picked up a small local puppy dog, the last one left in a litter of eight which had disappeared into nowhere as the days passed. I called her Pepper and picked her up in the rain as she was trying to feed herself with a plastic bag that contained the leftovers of some *rice and curry*.

I decided to take her home with me in the rainy season which often coincides with that of litters; little dogs roam everywhere and even though Sinhalese respect them, they often don't have the means to take care of them.

I also found Ginger one day, as she was walking in the middle of the main road and the tuk-tuks dodged her without even slowing down; she had a proud face, which meant she would always be strong and determined. Then came Garlik, who had followed me from the well to Wirdana; he was devastated by a severe lack of calcium and his legs were so twisted that they almost prevented him from walking. Despite his disability, he would try to run in an attempt to follow me every time I passed that way.

Unfortunately, the care and warmth I was able to give those puppies were not enough, so I decided to take them to Karla, in a faraway place where this Danish woman had put all her life savings to build a dog care centre to save stray dogs.

It was a clever project: they promised local families that they would take care of the small animals at a cost of 5,000 rupees a month. Stray dogs are a plague that afflicts many third world countries and she explained that she needed a lot of help to save her project, which was boycotted by the locals, who wondered why they needed to spend so much money just to save some animals.

Karla and I quickly became friends; I liked talking to her about our projects and every now and then we spent carefree evenings by the sea. We often liked to eat on Unawatuna beach and tell each other about our previous lives.

I had to leave Garlik there for a few weeks so he could get treatment, but I went to see him every day and took the opportunity to spend some time helping Karla.

In that period, I noticed that Sinhalese can sometimes be very cruel to animals and I didn't understand why. I had seen puppies being burned with boiling water, others constricted by metal wire with which they had been tied, dogs devastated by road accidents... the love with which those doctors and volunteers treated those little animals was incredible and made me think how men can be both cruel or, of course... fantastic.

CHAPTER 8

We had resumed building and towards the end of November we were almost ready to put on the roof.

While the foundations are indeed *fundamental*, the roof is perhaps even more so in a country where it rains 365 days a year. Taking shelter becomes more important than anything else.

We had to find a good carpenter for the roof, doors and windows; in theory it shouldn't have been a problem, given the amount of wonderful woods these people used. The wood lasts over time and becomes more and more beautiful. Over here, teak has a wonderful colour that isn't found anywhere else in the world. I had seen a lot of it in Thailand and Indonesia, yet the colour of Ceylon teak is completely different; kumbuk, which is comparable to our walnut, is fantastic, and iron wood, used to build the railways, is the hardest wood in the world. Then, there's ebony, which is still illegal in the country, but available at some antique dealers. They told me that in the northern region, in the Jaffna area, some craftsmen still used traditional methods.

I loved teak, only teak captures the sunlight, becomes that fantastic golden colour and improves with age; the core is black and gradually becomes lighter up until the outermost amber shades. That decision had been made and Sam introduced me to a young carpenter friend of his who lived in a house in the forest about twenty-five miles from Hikkaduwa.

I met Sughat and, as usual, it was difficult to explain what I wanted, but when he showed me some teak boards that he had just brought from the forest, we understood each other instantly. He explained that carpenters don't buy wood like we do back home, they go and get it straight from the forest, choosing the tree they want. It was fascinating stuff for someone like me, who was used to buying it already packaged from wholesalers.

I decided to go, too; it would be a new experience.

Going to get wood in the forest obviously implies having to sleep in the forest and live there for a while. Why not, I thought, after all, it's just a forest!

We organised everything so that we could leave that very same week. We would go sixty miles away, which required an entire day of travel, whereas at home the same distance would take just over an hour. I was more or less used to that by now, though.

I think, and I firmly believe, that the Sri Lankan jungles are some of the most beautiful green areas on Earth. Some of the plants are so beautiful that we Westerners would pay a hundred euros for a single leaf. Over here, they grow everywhere, as if they were arranged by a good landscape architect, next to each other. Ficus benjamin, bread trees, mangoes and palms of all kinds coexist. The rivers that run through the jungle are littered with large hanging rocks that look like they were placed there by giants, women still wash things and bathe in the streams, using bowls to wet their endlessly long hair.

The only human presence is represented by the white stupas of Buddhist temples that rise from the most beautiful places, as if put there by a higher force. Milk-white domes, ancient plasters, yoghurt and coral mixtures, where colourfully dressed monks stand out like characters from a cartoon.

Here in the forest, people sleep on trees, in small huts built on strong branches to protect themselves above all from elephants, who incredibly still roam free.

They are some of the most intelligent animals on the planet: the world of elephants is paradoxically so similar to that of humans and, inside the herds, the dynamics are more or less the same as in our societies.

Yet that impalpable world, made up of intertwining social bonds and which also touches upon complex emotions such as pain and suffering for the death of a close individual, is almost completely elusive to human beings who, at best, are content to attribute personal meanings to the gestures and "words" of others: but there are, and have always been, attempts to collect, catalogue and decode the recurring signals exchanged by these magnificent, majestic mammals, who are harmless and meek inhabitants of the savannahs and all too often the victims of ignorance and human wickedness that have turned them into mere "reserves" of ivory, to be killed when needed.

They explained to me and I learnt that their movements and gestures, which are incomprehensible to us, may constitute the most frequent forms of a language that elephants use to communicate with each other: things that can range from a slight touch of the trunk to a slight bend of an ear. Elephants are also excellent swimmers (the best of all land animals), their memory and intelligence are extraordinary, their longevity is comparable to that of humans, they have a sense of humour, they dream and are able to transmit knowledge. They cry and suffer when mistreated.

Fortunately, killing elephants in Sri Lanka is a crime punishable by the death penalty and they are considered sacred by the inhabitants of the island; they are venerated and decorated as deities.

However, the coexistence of humans and elephants in Sri Lanka is not a simple matter. Unfortunately, the growing proximity of humans and wild animals is the cause of increasingly frequent incidents: on the one hand, there are those who try to expand the amount land suited to cultivation, while on the other, the natural residents of the forest see the space available to them shrink more and more. In the wild, an elephant is driven by its instinct to defend its territory and its herd and this leads to the deaths of about fifty people every year, killed by charges of pachyderms that sometimes also destroy villages.

In the days of British rule, elephants were used to build railways... the British had spared no one! They had to dig deep holes and often refused because they often protect their newborns there.

They're not the only inhabitants of the forest.

There are snakes that curl up on trees like small lianas, insects as large as coconuts and small frogs in the most varied colours. Then, there are peacocks everywhere, small green parrots and much else.

Everything was dominated by the colour green; there were only a few flowers and even most of the birds were green, blue, turquoise or acid green. Even the worms were green, the chameleons became green, everything merged into that intense colour, which opened the eyes and the lungs.

There were no lights in the forest and, at night, the eyes have to slowly get used to the dark; the other senses develop incredibly, little by little the total darkness clears and the pupils begin to dilate to the point that they begin to see a little. Noises become more acute and if you concentrate deeply you can even hear the ants walking.

It was a great feeling, I wasn't afraid of that darkness and my mind was able to adapt. I began to feel safe in that tree house. How wrong could I be!

I woke up in the middle of the night with a strange sensation all over my body, like having pins stuck in me everywhere; I took a look at myself using a flashlight and saw huge blisters that were swelling up on my skin under my very eyes. One, ten, a hundred, as big as coins. My hands itched and had become thick and hard and my throat felt like someone was suffocating me.

I had a panic attack; I climbed down using the wooden ladder, there was only the guardian, who was sleeping. What could I do there, in the middle of nowhere? As soon as he saw me, he called the others and they immediately realised that I had to do something very quickly, immediately.

I understood once again that I had to trust them, I had to let them carry me away, perhaps to safety.

I could hardly breathe, I understood little and they talked agitatedly; they put me in Sam's old Jeep and we took a small road in the woods. The road climbed all the way up to a tiny village; it was almost morning when we got there.

They took me to a small house and kept repeating "clinic, clinic" to reassure me.

I remembered that I had read about small, very poisonous spiders that cause anaphylaxis in Nande's book. I thought we would find some cortisone, then I remembered that Neem oil is the most powerful natural antihistamine and cortisone.

We finally arrived and the doctor, a meek little man whose glasses I remember being the only thing that made him look like a specialist, began to analyse me and the blisters. I tried to explain about the spiders and the Neem, but I felt my strength leaving me. He looked at me in amazement, shaking his head, and it was the last thing I saw.

I woke up in the tree house covered in a yellow concoction and a blanket of leaves; there was a woman who smiled at me and simply said: "You are lucky, very lucky".

I was still feeling a fever and was told I had been asleep for two days. My hands were almost normal again, but every single muscle in my body hurt. I slept all day and only woke up to eat some red rice, drink its glutinous water and eat a bitter vegetable.

Three days had passed when I finally woke up properly: the fever had disappeared, the little doctor came to visit me and asked me how I knew all those things about spiders and Neem. He told me that he had used that information and that it had saved my life. So, I explained about the notebook; the story surprised him as much as it had surprised me.

The next day I got my strength back and once again took everything as a sign.

I thought about that specialist and how, one way or another, it was as though he had saved my life; there was a bond between me and that unknown friend that I was unable to understand, but one that grew with every passing day.

At that point, they had to find the carpenters, who had already cut down some trees, but I had to choose the ones that would be used for the large columns in the portico.

We didn't go far: there were so many trees! I thought about deforestation for a moment, about how long a tree takes to grow to that size and how little it took to cut it down. I asked if we could plant a small tree where we would cut them down and they laughed. How could I explain the value of what they had to those people?

They needed to look after their paradise.

Together with Thailand, Sri Lanka is the only country in the world where there are still rainforests that date back to prehistoric times. In Singaraja, in particular, there is a carnivorous plant with a flower that measures almost three and a half feet in diameter at certain times of the year.

I came up with a justification: basically, everything changes, or at least I liked to think so. Those trees would become the pillars of my project, the core of the building; their sacrifice would not have been in vain.

I was going mad, I thought, but my mind was changing slowly every day, as though guided by an invisible guru that was teaching it. Oh, how I had changed in such a short time! Nevertheless, I was happy with what I was becoming.

I had to get those thoughts out of my mind, we loaded the teak and headed back to Galle.

CHAPTER 9

After what had happened in the forest, I really wanted to use the tiles from Nande's old house as a small tribute; that sort of blanket that had protected the little house for so long gave me a sense of safety. I would also protect my little internal courtyard. Positioning those old tiles wasn't easy: it was a kind of layered warping that only a few elderly craftsmen still knew how to do.

Sam called an old labourer, an elderly gentleman who might have been a hundred years old or, more probably, around sixty. It was difficult to understand the age of the people there!

Some remain children, others grow old quickly, worn out by fatigue and the sun; there were women of my age who seemed old and young men who were already toothless or crooked with arthritis. Perhaps that was why, I had learned, that no one there asks your age, despite the thousands of other questions. It doesn't matter, people often die young.

In a country where life expectancy is sixty years, what matters is the present, partly because there will always be some other life after death.

In any event, the old man told me that he had always lived in the village and that he knew Nande. I was stunned: I could finally flesh out that figure that I had come to regard an indispensable presence a little more. He told me that Boussa used to be inhabited by people who had been deported after years in prison, one of the most famous in the country. That was what those long months of waiting written in the notebook meant!

After prison, the State gave these poor people jobs looking after the endless cinnamon plantations so that they could rebuild some sort of life.

He told me that no one knew much about Nande, calling him "the custodian of the fireflies". He was solitary and shy and no one had really grown to know him, they didn't understand what he really did, he was too cultured and refined to be a mere custodian. However, the old man knew that during the tsunami, despite his venerable age, he helped save lots of people and used his herbs to treat many of them for the infections that followed the cataclysm.

I asked if he knew more about his life, but he suddenly fell into a silence that I didn't understand at the time. I began to think that someone had to give me more detail: the book was just a diary with some faded photos, but it didn't contain any clear information.

Before he went silent, the old man had also told me that when Nande died, someone he knew had come in to remove his remains and had taken everything away. He asked why I was so interested in that solitary man, who everyone avoided.

This time, I was the one who fell silent: I didn't really know what to answer, so I used their own tactics.

On the last day of work on the roof, the man came to collect his wage, but before he left he delved into his crumpled sarong and pulled a package of papers that he said he would trade for three cigarettes. He told me that he had saved that package the day they took everything away.

I took the package and noticed that it contained new photographs and letters. That evening, I stayed at home to see what it contained. The first photo was of a group of people posing in front of what looked like a tea factory; the photo wasn't very clear, but there was a sign behind them: "Watawalla tea factory".

There were some locals and some Brits and I noticed a tall man among them who was much taller than the average. He had the most intense gaze I'd ever seen, with thick black eyebrows, a fleshy mouth and a proud air. It was him, it had to be. Nande.

The old man confirmed as much: it was him, Nande Wijesinghe, known in the village as "the custodian of the fireflies"!

For a second, the other people in the photo disappeared. I don't know if it's possible to connect this deeply with a ghost of sorts, but putting a face to Nande changed my life. I could actually imagine him walking around the garden with his long legs and a sarong worn down to his knees; I saw his long hands plucking leaves and planting Neem seeds, I imagined him praying with his hands clasped over his head, chewing betel, making paper lanterns for the holidays, preparing food with delicacies from his garden.

My respect for that man grew inside me with each passing day. I looked at the photo a thousand times: next to him were an English gentleman with a stern gaze and a young woman; her face was sad and she posed between the two men like a wax statue. She had an old-fashioned kind of beauty and her skin seemed even whiter, then I looked closer and noticed that her hands and feet were pointing towards Nande and not the man sitting next to her. I felt as if an invisible halo enveloped the two figures and separated them from the rest of the group.

Together with the photo that had caught my attention, the old man had given me an envelope with a letter inside. My legs were shaking. It was written in English.

My love,

My one great love, I can no longer bear the burden of this situation. Having you here and not being able to shout our love out to the world is killing me, day after day. They will hurt you and I cannot allow it, the baby I carry in my womb, the fruit of our love, will soon be born. I will have to leave the country, because he will kill me unless I do so.

The only solution is to run away together, away from here, far away where no one will be able to find us. I cannot and never will be able to live without you. Time passes quickly and we must be strong and ready. I am waiting for that day, my love, I count the days that divide us, but we must do it soon because I feel my strength seeping away.

I love you.

Yours forever,

Eileen

I was shivering: the woman in the photo was Eileen, it must have been her!

That was it, they loved each other, but what had really happened and why was the tone of the letter so sad? I also found a crumpled telegram in the envelope with just a few words:

"She has left us, but Gayan is with me".

Signed by a person called Tulsie.

It was a very common female name in Sri Lanka and I thought how complex it would be to track her down.

So, I assumed that Eileen had died during labour as she gave birth to their baby before they could run away together. The child, the fruit of their love, had probably been taken into care by a woman named Tulsie.

Adrenaline pushed my desire to sleep further and further away.

There were other payment receipts that I had already found in the notebook, but they were more clearly addressed to a place called Watawala, just a few rupees. Regular payments that Nande sent without skipping a month. Of course, he was in prison and then had to be deported; how could he see his son? Sending him some meagre savings was the only thing he could have done.

I thought about how I could find out more and perhaps get some news regarding the baby.

Perhaps in Watawala they would be able to tell me something about how he was imprisoned, probably accused by Eileen's family, no one could have accepted that intrusion into a respectable English family and, therefore, the best solution would have been to get rid of him by deporting him to a prison in the south of the country. That was how, at first in prison and then guarding the cinnamon plantation, he was estranged from Eileen and her life.

I was overcome with a veil of sadness and I told myself once again that I would try, if possible, to give meaning to his existence.

I convinced myself that I had to leave thing be for the time being… I still had a lot to do on my project.

I abandoned those thoughts and tried to settle down, but it was more difficult than expected.

I fell asleep thinking about Nande's story, which I couldn't get out of my head as I thought about how to continue my efforts on Wirdana.

CHAPTER 10

Work proceeded non-stop.

We worked all day until dark and I began to focus on what I thought might interest the types of tourists that would come from all corners of the globe. I wondered if everyone would love what I loved: who would appreciate that subtle beauty, that strange people, that discreet religion?

Many didn't even know where Sri Lanka was. Close to India? A region of India? Who knows! It wasn't the usual tourist destination, let alone seaside resort.

I made a list of things that travellers might enjoy and things that I could offer at Wirdana.

Nature, perhaps even more beautiful than Bali, beaches that easily rivalled those in Thailand, healthy, natural food, a millenary culture amputated by years of domination, which was nevertheless now returning to demand its dignity.

There was also an Ayurvedic tradition much older than the one in India, although some believe the opposite to be true; a country that was trying to pick itself up after years of war and shaken by a terrible tsunami. Yes, that country would offer the kind of enthusiasm of someone who knows that they hold a winning card. The opportunity of a life-time.

The more I wrote on my list, the more I forgot about all the negative things I had experienced and I realised that I had made a difficult choice, but that I was increasingly convinced that it was the right one.

I loved that people, I wanted them to understand that I felt like a guest, even if it was difficult for them to put the legacy of 300 years of colonisation and frustration to one side. For my part, I tried to draw a little closer to them every day.

Wirdana was taking shape and I liked how it was turning out. A place of peace, where anyone could feel at home; it was in my style, but the materials were all local, the colours were those of nature, of the land of tree trunks and palm trees. Colonial touches contrasting with modern shapes.

I decided to adopt the idea of the doors of Dutch buildings that open in four parts; light enters only from the top, preserving the intimacy inside the room. For the light fixtures, I had decided to use the large traps used by the fishermen, transforming them into lamps that would hang down from the ceiling.

I decided that elephants, which were also the national animal, had to somehow be part of Wirdana, so I decided to put large lithographs of photos that I had taken in the forest, life-size ones on the walls of the restaurant and in the private villas.

Teak furniture everywhere and a warm concrete floor, like the one I had also seen in Nande's house. I created a large pond with fish and lotus flowers in the heart of the building.

Thanks to Nande, the garden was an Eden of plants of all kinds and we could pick mangoes, oranges and jackfruit, the typical fruit of the country that we mistakenly call tropical tree.

I had thought of everything and I was finally beginning to see an end to the work. The result was almost out in the open and I loved it.

Sam managed the construction site; work was progressing well, of course, even if at times I felt a little lonely and often tired.

Since the work was coming to an end and my presence on site was no longer always necessary, I decided to take a break and took the opportunity to try and find Watawala. That thought, over the last few days, had never disappeared.

CHAPTER 11

I decided to rent an old 1950s Morris Minor car and Nirosh, with whom I had remained friends, offered to accompany me and be my driver.

The centre of the island was full of green hills covered in tea, which is still one of the island's main resources today. We didn't need to travel many miles, but the journey seemed interminable nevertheless.

I noticed that the roads throughout the country were oddly perfect, even in the middle of nowhere. As soon as you leave the coast and head inland, the blindingly green rice fields give way to cinnamon plantations, then coconut palms, rubber plants and, lastly, the tea hills appear.

The best thing about the route is that every mile street vendors offer what can be seen growing on the adjacent land, as if the road transforms into a large open-air market. I stopped to taste a fruit that was as hard as a cannonball, with a sour taste; at least eighteen kinds of red, lemon-flavoured or salted bananas… and eventually we stopped where the women sell the soft heart of the coconut, something I'd never seen before, like a big marshmallow that disappears in the mouth when you bite into it.

Nirosh explained that picking cashews was difficult: it's the national fruit. Cashews, she explained, come from a single red flower and are harvested one by one, which is why they're so expensive compared to the rest of the dried fruit on the market.

She showed me where they extract kitul, a kind of delicate honey that forms in the flower of a palm and is extracted little by little every day; the Sinhalese eat it with curd, a yogurt made from buffalo milk.

We crossed expanses of Neem trees and I remembered how those little yellow seeds had saved my life. The landscape then changed completely as we reached the area where the tea plantations began.

Tea covered the surrounding hills like a chenille blanket: small, short green plants that looked as though they had been lined up by a giant comb.

The harvesters, strictly women, worked like little red ants and appeared beyond the plants with their giant baskets; their skilful hands only took the buds of the plants to produce the finest tea and, at the end of the day, they were paid based on the amount of weight that they had picked.

They were strong women, hailing from Tamil Nadu, because the tradition of pickers was ancient and the British decided to bring in Tamils for this very purpose. When they took control of the island in 1798, the settlers had about a million Tamils transferred there and used them on tea plantations, since they were excellent workers and knew the language. The Tamils soon grew used to living in that land, which was so similar to their own country.

They reminded me of little cloth dolls that moved with precise, defined gestures; only they can collect the precious shoots because, even nowadays, there aren't any machines capable of doing so.

The work is well paid, they said; they left their villages to come and work here for 150 rupees a day, the equivalent of one euro. However, the more you work, the more you earn, and you can do so 360 days a year, without a break, which is why tea is big business: there are no seasons and it's produced all year round.

I tried to figure out where all that tea ended up and if it was owned by the British, who ruled there unchallenged. That thought immediately made me think of Nande.

I began to imagine what it must have been like during British rule; in the midst of the greenery still stood a few colonial bungalows which had stopped in time, small railway stations, little jewels, still with their timetables of the rare trains written in English. The scenery was breath-taking and a light misty frost covered the endless hills.

The landscape was even more beautiful than the one found on the coast.

We arrived in Nuwara Eliya in the evening, a town reminiscent of old England, with old British-style hotels, old clubs where women are not welcome, even now. I thought of Eileen, imprisoned in a world that wasn't her own... how she must have felt imprisoned in those crinolines? How could she live with a man she didn't love, dreaming of a life with Nande?

I fell asleep thinking of Eileen.

I got up early to see the sunrise: from the upland, covered in a thin mist, in the distance you could see Adams Peak, the sacred mountain in Sri Lanka, and expanses of tea interspersed with waterfalls that seemed to spring from the sky.

Nirosh told me that he had found the farm in Watawala, which was only a few miles away.

I was excited: we left immediately and arrived early; the women were loading the baskets to start the harvest and I waited outside on Nirosh's advice, who explained that it would be best if he spoke. I gave him the information I had and hoped someone still remembered Eileen.

He returned shortly afterwards with a slip of paper. He told me that the factory had been sold after the war and the owners had long since left. The first clue had gone, but I still had one hope: the transfers of money. Besides, maybe someone knew who that Tulsie was in Watawala.

The town was practically inexistent: it consisted of a few houses along the road, some buildings that climbed up the mountain, pine trees and the tracks of a railway that perhaps connected it to the outside world. We asked if anyone knew Tulsie and that unlikely address in the town shop; people shook their heads, someone gave directions that were soon contradicted, as I was used to seeing. I decided to go to the school, where perhaps someone knew something about Gayan. Then, with Nirosh's help, I found a small green building in the middle of a clearing. Once again, I let Nirosh go inside; my language and my status prevented me from communicating easily.

Nirosh got back in the car with a triumphant air and told me that maybe we had found Tulsie.

My eyes opened wide.

We left the car and climbed up a small path towards the tracks, among the brushwood and leeches, a real menace in mountain villages. The stones were slippery, but we eventually saw a house at the end of the path. We stopped at the sight of the train, a small blue train that carried the few tourists from the coast to Nuwara Eliya.

There was no one home, but the embers of the fire were still warm and the remains of a frugal meal were still there. The view was fantastic: valleys strewn with pine trees, gardens of scallions and gumba (so-called ladyfingers) all around. I looked closer and saw a woman bent down as she worked in the garden: when she saw me, she continued to work, bending down again as if I were not even there ("those who don't ask get no answers", as the usual Sinhalese saying goes).

I went down the slope and sat down on a stone next to her.

She looked like she was a hundred years old, but her eyes were as lively as a child's, although fatigue had consumed her. She didn't speak English, I understood that right away. She put down her spade and sat down on a rock next to me.

"Nande Wijesinghe", I limited myself to saying.

She looked at me suspiciously, then she motioned to follow her; we went into the house and she made me sit in a plastic chair near the kitchen while she made tea without speaking. I hoped that Nirosh, who was talking to the villagers for information, would arrive soon. The scent of tea intoxicated the room.

I waited for her slow, precise movements to finish and for her to make up her mind to talk to me, so I held out the photo in an attempt to get her attention, but she didn't even look at it and left the room.

Nirosh came in shortly afterwards and I heard them talking; she then came back to me holding a small box and took out a photo of a beautiful child: his eyes were like Nande's, his eyebrows were black, but his skin was light. She showed me a photo of a tall boy with coarse black hair, but the proud air of his father and Eileen's features.

There was a photo in the local school: it was of Gayan proudly wearing his uniform.

Tulsie said something in her language, then she began to cry; I didn't understand what she was saying, but I understood that she was referring to something like "army". There was a photo of the boy in attack gear.

"Gayan", she said, before beginning to cry again.

Nirosh told me that she had not heard from Gayan again and that he was considered missing in Trincomalee after a bloody reprisal in 1982. That was the last she'd heard.

I saw Tulsie talking to Nirosh and the man then drew close to me: "She's tired now. Go outside, I'll join you in a minute".

I went out the back of the house while Nirosh tried to calm her down; in that instant, a train passed with some tourists who were looking out of the window at that little corner of the world where people would never think of stopping. It's one of those places that you catch a glimpse of when passing quickly: just a postcard for most people.

I tried to reconstruct the story in my head.

I didn't have much information to go on, Nande's story stopped on the day when his son was declared missing in one of the battles of a bloody, endless war.

Tulsie had told Nirosh that the young man had left to join the garrison in Trincomalee because there were no other opportunities to make a future for himself, as was the case for so many young people at the time. Many years had since passed and a Sinhalese person from the mountains, worse still a woman, simply could not cross the country to look for someone she hadn't heard from for years. More than ever, I now felt that it would also be important to find something for that woman, who had taken care of the boy for so long.

It was as if the story had come full circle once again.

Now everything was a little clearer: since the death of his mother, little Gayan had been placed in the care of Tulsie, because no one in the family would take care of a half-caste child, especially the son of a clandestine relationship; a little bastard who could have no ties to English nobility. Nande hadn't been able to do anything for him, because he had immediately been expelled from the plantation, investigated and deported to Boussa. He had rebuilt his life and worked hard so that he could give little Gayan the support he needed with his poor means. The only job opportunity, for a former convict, was to work in the cinnamon plantations in the south, which happened to be something he was good at. At a certain point, he'd stopped getting updates regarding his son and that was where my information had also ground to a halt.

I thought of how much that man must have suffered!

It was time to go back and I didn't talk much in the car, I kept thinking about that story.

Eileen had died in childbirth giving birth to Nande's son, the child she was placed into care and Nande was deported... then came the tragedy of the war. It couldn't end like that, it shouldn't end like that.

Maybe I could find out more, why not give it a try? I owed it to Nande, who unknowingly and indirectly helped me with the project based on his house and who, moreover, had saved my life, thanks to his knowledge.

It was as if the story had enveloped me in an invisible net from which I was still unable to free myself. When the weather improved, I decided I would pay a visit to Trincomalee, a town in the north on the east coast, the last bastion of the civil war, to find information regarding the young Gayan.

CHAPTER 12

It was time to decide on the furnishings.

I had been to all the shops in Colombo and the antique dealers in Kandy; I liked the colonial style a lot, but I also wanted something different. During my years in Bali, I had discovered hidden places and special craftsmen and I knew that was where I could easily find everything I was looking for, so I decided it was time for a break from that whirlwind of events and go back there.

I wanted to see some friends again and enjoy the social life a little.

I found everything as I had left it: there was a little more in turmoil each time, but it was still my Bali. Sebastian came to pick me up at the airport; he was a dear friend who had been living on the island for lots of years and was now in charge of international shipping. He had an engaging, odd way of speaking English and had always made me feel very happy.

He had a small house near Canggu on a beach with black sand where surfers rode the waves on one of the most popular breaks in the world. I found myself thinking about my little tear and how much time had passed since the last time I had tasted a piece of social life.

Two small islands, Bali and Sri Lanka, which are very similar in some ways. Separated by a difference of thirty years of tourism, of course. It was only then that I grasped all the differences and similarities and saw everything in a new light.

The morning following my arrival, Sebastian and I decided to rent a motorbike to get around the island a little easier. Traffic was nearly ten times that in Sri Lanka; there were thousands of motorbikes and they moved around the island like ants, honking and trumpeting continuously.

The Balinese have learned to live with tourism for many years, they respect and know about foreigners; in the land of frogs, on the other hand, the recent sporadic form of tourism means that the Sinhalese still consider it something that should be "exploited": quickly and immediately, often without thinking about the consequences that reckless behaviour could cause in the long term.

I knew it wasn't always the case, but I had heard stories in Sri Lanka about people who had suffered petty scams or swindle, even now.

I met many artisans during those days, all over the island, buying rattan rugs, furniture, pots, handles and anything that might embellish Wirdana. I was spoiled for choice and had forgotten about the flurry of wonderful lamps, baskets and sculptures. Every corner hosted a succession of craftsmen who produced all sorts of things and more.

Sebastian knew how to negotiate and go around the little shops discovering the most particular things. We had worked together for many years and we understood each other. It was fun and the most exciting moment of my project, the best part after so much effort, had finally arrived.

We had long chats on the beach as we strolled along the shoreline; the sea was cold there, not like the Indian ocean... the Pacific was very different. At low tide, the women gathered the sea urchins and shells and the tanned surfers rode the giant waves. The sunsets on the beach were incredible and the silhouettes of a thousand kites, which flew in the skies above Bali in that period, looked like flocks of birds carried by the wind. Sipping a Mojito on Berawa beach, filled with tourists and surfers from all over the world, made me think a little about Baradise beach and the silence of that pristine place.

After a few days, we agreed that we both wanted to get away from the hustle and bustle of the coast to look for something different.

I already knew that landing in Bali meant entering a magical bubble in which anything could happen, as if in a dream, but to make certain coincidences or particular situations happen, you truly need to go with the flow and your own sixth sense.

I considered it a small corner of tropical paradise, where Hindu temples alternated with expanses of rice fields and mile-long beaches of white sand. That was Bali or, rather, an ideal depiction of it that didn't always correspond to the truth. The reality of that small Indonesian island was much more complex than it seemed and had undergone many, obvious changes over the years in the eyes of those who knew what it used to be like.

Back in the day, buildings were no taller than coconut trees, connected by a few roads and surrounded by rice fields. There were also very few cars and the main means of transport was the bicycle, women still washed themselves in the rivers and the ceremonies in remote villages gave the island its ancestral splendour.

While still considering it unique and special, I was aware that the gentrification it had suffered due to tourism had stripped it of many of its beauties. However, the local population had been able to manage the phenomenon of the immigration of people and capital in great quantities, which struck their small island with overwhelming force, transforming it into an economic and social powerhouse, without compromising the cultural core of the island. Perhaps that represented Bali's greatest strength, destined to always maintain its own identity, despite the additional layers of concrete and smog that began to accumulate.

Ubud was still without doubt my favourite place. It had become famous over the years as a meeting place for lovers of holistic, spiritual and supernatural procedures; even now, you can take part in the numerous spiritual rites that are held around the city.

I wanted to relive the sense of peace that I had felt many years before and that I had also experienced with the help of Nande in Ceylon, so I looked for the right place for my new purification.

Melukat is one of the most important purification rituals in the Balinese tradition, which can be performed whenever you feel that something is blocking your energy. There are very few sacred temples dedicated to Melukat and the rite can be done individually, although usually, especially for us Westerners, it's best done with a healing priest guiding you on one of the strongest paths of your life. However, as happens with spiritual paths, you're not the one who finds the priest, it's the priest who finds you.

With Sebastian's help, I soon found my Balian, a traditional healer from Bali; some of them receive their powers as an innate gift, others from the study of Balinese Hindu philosophy and others still through a long and intense initiation period by a more experienced healer.

Mine was called Cokorda Rai.

He performed traditional Balinese practices, treating both physical and mental illnesses through the use of various therapies, natural herbs and ancient wisdom; he used various pressure point techniques to analyse physical problems or emotional stress, gave instructions for the future and general advice.

After a long wait in a queue made up of locals and a few curious tourists, my time had come, so I climbed onto a platform under an alang alang roof and knelt in front of Mr Rai.

"What seems to be the problem?", he asked me in Bahasa, a language I knew very well.

What was my problem?

I only told him that I often felt lost, that I was afraid of the future and often didn't know where to go. He looked at me with a friendly toothless smile and started his procedure.

His treatment was very physical. Firstly, he made me lie down on a bed of straw and then began praying while facing his handcrafted temple. After the prayer, he came towards me and began to probe my abdominal area in order to understand if there were any tensions or knots and immediately began to dissolve them with great precision and strength.

Lastly, he began the part where he told me what I should do and predicted what would happen to me.

"Listen carefully...", he said, "you need to wake up as a new person every day. Experiencing a new world every day. Only then will you find the answers!"

I was a little disappointed by that one sentence, because I wanted someone to give me some clear answers. I wanted someone to tell me that the future was guaranteed, far better than the current situation. It makes life so much easier knowing that whatever we are going through now is a temporary stop along the way to making things better for the future... it applies to everyone.

Yes, uncertainty surrounding the future scared me. However, at the same time, I realised that that was what made life interesting.

So, I concluded that what Cokorda Rai was suggesting in terms of waking up as a new person wasn't bad advice after all. Indeed, we should face each morning as if we've never seen it before. Tackling every day, every problem, every struggle with the strength and enthusiasm of the first day.

I realised how many times I'd had my future read, I'd met healers, fortune tellers, shamans and gurus of all kinds in the most disparate parts of the earth. I had even done so a few months earlier in Galle, where there was a shaman who looked at a full glass of lotus water and predicted your fate by reading its bubbles, even telling you on what day you would die. Why had I done it? What was it for?

Instead, I decided to savour life without knowing all the answers and take a difficult moment for what it was, run with it, grasp it, process everything I was experiencing in the present. It would be a much wiser course of action.

Now immersed in the mysticism of the island, we decided to climb Mount Batur, the highest and most revered mountain in Bali, on a day with a full moon. Measuring 10,208 feet high, it can be seen from most parts of the island, although it's often covered by clouds and a persistent mist. It's still an active volcano: its last, violent eruption in 1963 spared the Mother Besakih temple, which is located on its slopes, by a few yards and miraculously avoided the communities where some of Bali's shamans, those who mend bones, wizards of rain and wind, who use their powers to control the force of the volcano, and the Balians who specialise in love potions still live.

The event was considered miraculous and since then the Balinese have not ceased to venerate both the temple and the volcano, making continuous pilgrimages and offers of flowers.

We hadn't planned to climb to the top of the mountain, but its beauty, its sacredness and the words full of respect and veneration with which it is described made us change our minds. I had immerse myself in sensations as long as possible, so why not go up the steep paths that led to the top, contemplating the world on the edge of a crater, poised between heaven and hell?

The volcano, as per tradition, was climbed at night to have the thrill of seeing the sunrise from the summit, the only time of day when the volcano is certain to be free from the clouds.

We left at midnight and the sky was starry; it was a magical night. Our guide was waiting for us at the Pasar Agung monastery, where the path that climbs the volcano begins: to our surprise, it was a young woman with long hair and a backpack that was bigger than she was. She often stopped to light incense and put flowers in small temples along the way.

"So that the mountain spirits will help us", she explained.

Hence, the spiritual climb began on a night overflowing with stars and with a full moon, while in the background the contours of the island could be seen clearly, illuminated by the thousand lights of the cities.

After four hours of walking, we reached the lower edge of the crater, where we met other tourists who had probably left before us. It was dawn and, below us, the volcano projected a pyramid of shadow that obscured half of Bali. It was a truly emotional moment.

We were close enough to touch the clouds. We took time to enjoy the sunrise and the early hours of the morning; when we began our descent, the sun was already high. We no longer needed an electric torch, we could easily see the steep, slippery rock and we understood the feat we had accomplished during the night, almost without realising it.

Upon arrival, we were exhausted, yet happy. We thanked the spirits of the mountain for making us return safe and sound: those of the volcano for not inundating us, the rocks for making us strong, the trees for providing a roof over our heads, the wind for pushing us upwards and the stars for illuminating the path.

That was not our last experience: we left for Nusa Lembongan, where many friends had settled in the past, rebuilding there what they had been looking for many years earlier. The islands around Bali, once deserted and believed to be inhabited by spirits and demons, are amazing and just a few hours by boat are needed to reach wonderful places where expats, tired of the chaos in the south, have moved, creating new colonies of alternative Bohemians.

Peter, a friend, had been living on the island for several years and had begun his work collecting and breeding cosmetic seaweeds that were now sold as elixirs in Japan and Korea, where they were all the rage. He'd made a real business out of it and now acted like a true entrepreneur, arguing that algae, like insects, would be the sole next source of human sustenance.

Lorna, on the other hand, had continued her yoga retreats and dozens of people went there every year to purify themselves from the frenzy of civilisation, but I no longer recognised my old, dear yoga, because now it was called in many different ways that evoked ecstatic wonders, such as "blissful sound healing", "vocal alchemy" and "warm water heater meditation".

There was also the renowned "Ecstatic dance", a sort of trance in which dancing bodies melt into oblivion. Lorna explained that it was a global movement that was active in more than a hundred cities around the world and started in Bali.

Then, there were some who had opened Bio-Evolutionary cuisine restaurants, Locavore that only eat food produced less than ten miles away. They are followers of local food consumption, which is a bit complicated to implement, but undoubtedly commendable.

That wasn't all: there were also "Respirians" who, instead, live on breath and light alone. During their meditation phases, they absorb "prana", a scientifically unproven molecule that seemingly appears in their mouths as if by magic. Inexplicably, Respirians are very thin and lack vitality. Indeed, this category of people is uncommon, since it can only be reached after a spiritual journey and proper preparation, which even to me, despite considering myself quite open, was unknown.

I later discovered that some friends of mine had founded a community of "Raelians". This had something to do with the Elohim and the circle of light; it seems that the latter are extraterrestrial creatures that disappeared into the cosmos immediately after creating us, about 35,000 years ago. Apparently, the aliens are waiting for their earthly "children" to build an embassy to welcome them. Folkloristic, but undoubtedly commendable in terms of foresight.

These forms of fundamentalism and bizarre movements led me to make a reflection: I, who had always been, and still am, a "simple vegetarian", realised that vegetarians and vegans were not only seen as people who had chosen not to eat meat or products derived from animals, but people who had also embraced an entire system of thought that made them quite naïve in the eyes of others: conspiracy theorists, anti-capitalists, yoga practitioners, incense consumers and gluttons for breaths!

In truth, many vegetarians are none of those. They simply love nature, genuine flavours, animals and the environment. Above all, they don't think that anyone who eats meat is necessarily a "serial killer", but perhaps just has a different way of thinking that should be respected.

It made me smile that whatever took you to that island, away from sinister consumerism and away from the busy life of the West, had a magical effect and anyone who came this far was immersed in a reality that made them feel like a hippy from the sixties or, better still, an ascetic.

That was also part of Bali and why not, after all? We all wanted to escape and build a new identity to make us feel free for the time we would be away.

Sebastian agreed with me that, nevertheless, if you really want to experience the genuine essence of Bali, you had to go to its most remote places, such as its western edge, where we decided to go on our motorcycle.

We crossed the whole island to get to the western side, where the wildest area of the island, which had become a national park, was located. Deserted beaches, unlike the crowded ones in the south.

Here, deer and fawn strolled freely and the sea was teeming with tropical fish and coral reefs of pristine beauty; we stopped at a small hotel on the beach overlooking the island of Manjangaan, famous for its wonderful corals.

Lots of wild animals in that remote area still live in their natural habitat.

The magic of that place, lit by a moon that made the silver sea sparkle, was unique. We swam in the moonlight and savoured that pristine wonder. On the way back, we made a stop in Lovina, a quiet town on the north coast where the sea was calm. There we found undisturbed colonies of dolphins with which you can swim in an unforgettable experience. I was told that a famous shaman, who had built his home on a source of water that was apparently miraculous, lived not far from there. We decided to join him and experience that purifying bath. Bali is filled with springs of sulphurous, warm water where the locals purify themselves.

Before an important event, when you bathe in that water with extraordinary powers, it's like your head and then your body immerse themselves in another dimension and you seem to come out with your mind purified of bad thoughts and fears. That was the exact sensation I got back then.

As much as I knew that Bali would give me a lot and that it would be an extraordinary adventure, I never imagined experiencing such strong emotions again. I thought back to my new life and the wonderful places I had discovered in recent years... it was a bit like a reward for what I had been through.

I spent the days in constant gratitude thanking the Universe for everything that it was giving me, something that really was priceless and that couldn't be bought with any currency known to man, but only by opening the heart to life, with new ever brighter eyes and an increasingly open mind... wide open, I dare say!

I gave thanks every minute of the wild life that had enchanted me and the events that I continued to face with great enthusiasm.

So it was that I rediscovered Bali in all its new facets. Of course, modern times had partly distorted its charm, suffocated by a crowd that flees from other latitudes and goes there to seek, if it's able to find it, freedom and its essence. A small casket unfortunately destined to disappear in the future, a Hindu enclave in a world blessed by Allah that is about to devour it.

It tries to defend itself with its thousands of temples, which are far more opulent than those in Sri Lanka, with its luxuriant nature that seems to want to take back its space as soon as possible, transforming its integrity into a paradise for those who want to find their inner self.

The thing that hadn't changed and that I'd always liked were the Balinese people who, with their smiles and gestures, offered a spectacle to those arriving from the West every single day. They were all happy, thousands of smiles... after all, how could they not be? They had never experienced wars or cataclysms and had even been spared by the tsunami, despite being much closer to the epicentre of the earthquake.

It's as if Bali was the lucky little sister of Sri Lanka, very similar in many ways, the same waves, endless beaches, untamed nature... yet, even though I loved these places, my heart and my thoughts took me back to my sad little island.

I told myself that Bali had had its time, I was leaving it now like you would a grown son who is able to live on his own, while my little "tear" still needed me.

I knew that it would soon happen there, too: the days of all these paradises are numbered, but Sri Lanka still had some time left for me. Perhaps it wouldn't end up evolving very quickly, but that would depend on many things, even though no one could tell how long it would take.

We spent the last few days peacefully, wandering around and working to find everything I needed for Wirdana; I would bring back pieces of that stimulating, vital place with me and embellished my refuge with the essence of Bali.

Soon it was time to leave: a month had already passed.

After all, we had already bought and packed everything, my work was finished and it was time to go back. Sebastian told me that he would soon come and visit me in Sri Lanka; he accompanied me to Denpasar, in the midst of the thousand lights and the fast-moving cars.

We hugged, as always, then I said goodbye to that precious friend and boarded the plane for Colombo.

CHAPTER 13

I had a strange sensation, as often happens.

When I left Denpasar airport, I had a feeling that my return was not going to be easy.

My local phone hadn't worked for over a month, I hadn't received any messages or phone calls and I knew next to nothing of what had happened at Wirdana. I landed in Colombo on 10 February 2017.

The immigration officer smiled at me, checked my visa as usual, then started flipping through the computer, began to fidget and called a colleague from the passport office. I didn't understand why: my visa was valid until April.

Three men in uniform arrived and I realised that two of them were policemen, then one of them kindly asked me to follow him to the office. I thought there must be a problem with my luggage, which was full of small pieces of furniture... perhaps I'd gone over the permitted weight?

I went into the office and they made me sit down.

"Big problem, madam", one of the policemen said. He didn't speak good English, but I began to understand that something was wrong. In my worst nightmares, as a traveller, there were episodes of *Banged Up Abroad*, a programme in which unsuspecting foreigners found themselves embroiled in drug issues or illegal exports. I began to feel uncomfortable and my mind went to the episode in which two girls in Bangkok, who had had drugs placed in their luggage, were arrested and spent more than five hellish years in a Thai prison.

It's best not to have these types of problems in a country such as this one. However, I'd never lost sight of my suitcase since I'd arrived at Denpasar airport.

After about half an hour of the usual incomprehensible discussions, a woman in uniform arrived and told me that we had to go to Galle. I started asking for an explanation, but I'd learnt that if they're not inclined to do so, no one would give you an explanation. I was tired from the journey and gave in to that way of doing things.

They took me from one office to another, then eventually put me in an old police van and we left the airport heading south.

We took the Galle motorway exit and headed in a direction that was very familiar to me. Nobody spoke in the car; or, rather, they were speaking in their language, which I found more difficult to understand than ever.

We arrived in Boussa and I thought they would accompany me home, but we passed the exit leading to Wirdana; I knew those roads well, we also passed the "Water for elephant", the army camp and stopped in front of the Boussa penitentiary.

I knew that it was one of the main prisons on the coast and that was the place where some of the leaders of the Tamil rebels, the famous Tamil tigers, who had been arrested after the genocide at the end of the civil war, were still held.

We stopped in front of the gate. Were they going to take me in there? It was a nightmare and I couldn't even understand what was going on.

They took me to another office, if you could call it that; inside, some men in uniform "welcomed us" and, finally, a man who seemed to speak good English arrived. They were kind enough, all told. Good-natured smiles and indecipherable looks.

"Big problem", he also said, before explaining what had happened.

A few months earlier, I had given don Shane a cheque to pay for the land and he had signed it over to another person who, in turn, had signed it over to a fourth; it was only 9,000 euros, which is little for a European, but enough over here to spark a big dispute.

He told me that the cheque had bounced and that the person who tried to cash it was not exactly the reasonable type. I smiled and said that there must have been a mistake and that I would speak to my lawyer and resolve the situation that same day.

Unfortunately, he explained that it wasn't that simple.

He told me that the law stipulated that I would have to remain in prison until it was cashed and that, as a resident of the country, I would have to strictly abide by the rules.

Unfortunately, during the time I was away, the person in question had filed a complaint and had set in motion a succession of complications that could no longer be stopped. I turned on my telephone and found a myriad of messages from my lawyer and other numbers I didn't recognise. I asked to call my lawyer in Colombo, but it was evening by now and he didn't answer the telephone. Before I could call Sam, they took my mobile phone and told me I would have to wait until the next day.

Not in a million years! I said I lived nearby and could go home and come back the next morning. I was given a stern look.

"Maybe you haven't understood properly", he told me in English.

I had to spend the night in there. I tried to reason with them, but they started speaking Sinhala and I became invisible. I remembered tales I had heard, stories of the law that still punished adulteresses and cherry thieves.

I had tears in my throat, but I didn't want to give those people the idea that I was even more helpless than I already was. The next day seemed such a long way away! A short period of time that stretched out of proportion in that situation, becoming incalculable. And then, what would happen the next day? Naturally, I would call my lawyer and he would resolve everything ... I tried to stay calm and thought that, after all, it was only a few hours.

With no mobile phone or answers, everything became absurd in there; I remembered the advice I had heard about not speaking of this to anyone, so that's what I did. As they took me away, I thought that Nande must have been in there for years and I felt he was close to me again. That thought gave me strength.

The women's "section" of the Boussa prison was very small and located in a building just outside the men's section. There aren't many female criminals there given the social conditions in which they live; there are also very few prostitutes since the Buddhist religion forbids the practice. Few murderers (they usually kill themselves), but there were some thieves: hunger would sometimes transform them into criminals.

I had often seen places like this in the alleyways in Colombo or on the outskirts of Galle: peeling hovels with ramshackle camp beds, flashing neon lamps and filth everywhere.

The policewoman was nice, all in all; she took me to a room where there were two showers and asked me to take off my clothes. I didn't even consider doing so! Taking off my clothes meant stripping me of what little dignity I had left. I managed to persuade her and we walked down a small corridor which overlooked some small rooms divided only by curtains, as was also the case in Sinhalese homes.

She then she made me "take" one of them. There was nobody else there. She showed me a bathroom and left. I sat down on the camp bed and told myself that if I slept the time would pass quickly.

I took off my jacket, placed it under my head and closed my eyes for a while. I couldn't sleep: I was angry and dazed, even if for a minute I almost laughed at the absurdity of the situation.

I didn't even have a watch.

I began my meditation exercises to avoid thinking and fell into a state of mind that I cannot explain. I came back to my senses when I felt I was being observed by black eyes staring at me: it was a young girl, she couldn't have been more than eighteen. She was touching my hair; I got up quickly and she went away frightened.

As expected, she didn't speak a word of English; she was stunningly beautiful and I couldn't understand how such a creature could be in a place like that, but I was also there, after all, so once again I found myself thinking that few things make sense to us in that country.

As I was lost in my thoughts, the guard called us for dinner. I wasn't hungry, how could I even think about eating? The girl took me by the hand and we went to a room where there were about ten people.

The scene was similar to the ones I had already seen a number of times, it looked like a home reunion. Among the black braids, I saw a woman of about sixty who looked European despite the fact that she wore a braid that was typical of Sinhalese women, so I instinctively approached her.

She wasn't as friendly as I was hoping for and she said a few words in Sinhala: she had huge tattoos all over her body, she was tall, very thin and had a very hard face.

She only uttered a few words in English after she had finished eating. She told me that she was Hungarian, even though she'd lived her life in India; I asked her how long she'd been in there and when she replied that it had been three years, I almost fainted.

I told her that I would be out the next day and she gave me a slight smile. I asked her if she had received any special treatment.

"Haven't you understood this country, yet?", she replied.

She said her name was Nede and decided to tell me her story, maintaining a distant air, as if she didn't trust anyone, but perhaps she had seen something in me that made her a little more conciliatory.

She told me that she had lived in Rishikesh for ten years, in an Ashram on the banks of the Ganges, an incredible place on the slopes of the Himalayas where that great river is born and then goes down to the valley and crosses all of India.

The city is dotted with dozens of Ashrams, where hundreds of hippies from the 2000s took refuge and mingled with the Shadu, who have lived there for decades. She had left Hungary like many other Western spiritual seekers... the Beatles had also lived there for about two months to meditate with their guru Maharishi baba.

A long suspension bridge divides two worlds: chaotic India and traffic on one side, spiritual India on the other. Pilgrims bathe in the Ganges to regain their cosmic awareness, recognising the power of various drugs to fill existential voids and experience wonderful journeys, all fleeing the consumerism of modern life.

Some were rich and famous like, others like Nede, who were simply in pain and in need of finding their place in the world. They came here to "relate intimately with the other stages of their consciousness". So said Nede.

She used hashish, marijuana, LSD... she said that marijuana is also widely used in Sri Lanka, indeed legally in Ayurveda, but it is very different and lighter. For the one that really gets you high, you had to use the one from India, cut with many other substances.

One day in Rishikesh, her pushers had offered her a deal: she would transport a shipment of drugs to Colombo and then from there to the transgressive beach of Hikkaduwa. It would be very straightforward. A two-hour flight was all it would take.

"Why not? I thought. What did I have to lose? I began the journey with two kilos of hashish hidden in a Ganesh figurine, specially packaged for easy transportation".

Unfortunately, she said, either because of her bizarre appearance or just bad luck, Nede found herself dealing with the local police. The penalties importing drugs into Sri Lanka are very severe; even though the death penalty had recently been abolished, she was sentenced to twenty years in prison.

She didn't seem so upset... almost as though nothing could touch her that much. She had quickly adapted to that life, in prison she had quickly become a sort of boss, she pretty much got everything she asked for and even managed to get some marijuana. Absurd and inconsistent, but as I had long understood, nothing here really made much sense. After all, she told me, her life wasn't all that different from the one in the Ashram and, in any case, her lawyer would get her out in about ten years.

She finished her story and dismissed me with the usual coldness. She began to smoke without taking any further notice of me.

Nede's story had distracted me away for a while; I didn't even touch the food, I felt nauseous and we went back to the room. The girl didn't speak, she looked at the window. I walked over and asked her who she was. We couldn't communicate well, but Nede spoke perfect Sinhala and I thought she might help me understand what the young woman had to say, so we went back to the common room that was still open to the inmates.

Although she didn't seem happy to do so, Nede accepted my request and translated what Sampatha, which was what the girl called herself, said.

She was born in a village in the Badulla district, her mother left at a young age to go and work in the east. She lived with her younger siblings and a sick father, struck down by diabetes that had rendered him disabled. The village was very small, but she'd met a nice boy, Sange, who didn't have a stable job and his family was even poorer than hers. They loved each other, but their love, as often happens, was hampered by not being able to marry because of her family, who wanted her to wed a richer man.

One day, her father told her that she had been promised to a man in a nearby district and that the families would meet soon to decide the wedding day.

Sampatha tried to talk to Sange to explain, but her cousins had kept him away.

The girl had been prepared for the meeting of the families and they had made her wear a turquoise sari, they had put henna make up on her, as was the custom on the day of an engagement, and they had dressed her up like a rag doll.

That morning, Sange had run to her small house to try to see and talk to her, but they had turned him away once again. Locked up in the house, she tried to see the face of the man who would soon become her husband from the window.

They took her outside when everyone else was already seated: they had set up a few plastic chairs in the courtyard and the aunts had made sweets and Chai tea, as is customary on special occasions.

The man had a severe air about him and must have been over fifty years old. Sampatha sat down with a lump in her throat, the man spoke only to her father and didn't even glance at her. Soon, the women withdrew, including Sampatha, and the men of the family remained to discuss the details and decide the wedding date.

In her room, the young woman thought of what she had always dreamed of: crowning her love with Sange. Her big dream was gone, tears flooded her face and she felt like dying.

In Sri Lanka, no one can refuse a decision of the family and can only resign themselves to their sad fate; some luckier ones learn to love each other, but many accept a life without love.

It's hard for us to understand, but in India once they told me it's not that bad; couples married by proxy sometimes learn to love each other over time and the average number of arranged marriages that work is often higher than those that take place out of love!

The following morning, some boys from the village went to warn Sampatha that Sange had taken his own life during the night by drinking rat poison. In that moment, the girl also felt like dying and she remained locked in the house for a month almost without eating: she drank and nibbled only what was necessary for her to stay alive. Her father told her that they had no other choice and that the man was well off and would take care of her and the whole family.

Shortly thereafter, the day of the wedding came, the day that all girls dream of, especially here. Families often go into debt to be able to celebrate a dignified wedding and, for many, the dream of feeling like princes and princesses for a day comes true.

The sumptuous dresses and hairdos are a pageant of sequins and silks and the wedding photos often remain on display in houses as the trophy of a life-time: one day in paradise, no longer beggars, but kings and queens of a dream that vanishes the following day.

It wasn't even that for Sampatha.

That day, she was beautiful as usual, in a cream-coloured dress covered in pearls, on her head a chain of small rhinestones framed her porcelain face, made up like a doll.

She spent the entire ceremony with her eyes wide open and her face expressionless. That night, she found herself with that unknown man for the first time, he didn't speak to her and took her roughly, taking what she had held most dear with violent, indelicate gestures.

Sampatha died inside once again.

The next day, with her meagre luggage, she had to move into his house five hours away from her village, with her old mother-in-law and his brothers.

He soon showed himself to be a violent man, he drank often and beat her for no reason; he dragged her around her house by her long hair, forcing her to submit to him wishes.

One night, Sampatha tried to escape; even though she didn't know where to go, he woke up and beat her like he had never done before. So, the girl took a large knife from the kitchen and stabbed him as many times as she could, until the man fell lifeless into a pool of blood.

The court was lenient, all told, given the man's previous record, and she was eventually sentenced to 30 years. Sampatha had tried to commit suicide in prison several times, but the guards had stopped her.

My heart ached: that little girl was nineteen and she still had another twenty-nine years left in there. I didn't know what to say, she stroked me and smiled; she said I needn't worry. I couldn't get my head around it: how could such situations still exist in 2017? And yet, I knew that similar cases were very common in Arab countries and in much of the East. Conditions for women are still shameful and no one does anything to try and change them.

Sampatha then told us that Sange's ghost comes to visit her at night and it was the only thing that kept her alive. I didn't say anything so as not to upset her any more: I knew that Sinhalese believe in ghosts a lot and communicate with them often, as if they were real; it's a very widespread belief and that's why they haven't burned bodies for a long time.

We went back to the "cell" in the middle of the night and I tried not to think too much and fall asleep.

That night I had the worst nightmares of my life.

I dreamt of Sampatha covered in blood, Eileen screaming, Nande being dragged to prison and myself under a very tall wave that was about to overwhelm me. I waited under the wave to be overwhelmed, but when the impact was about to take place, I woke up with a start.

There was a little light; it must have been around six. I got ready, certain that the nightmare would end soon and someone would come and get me out.

I waited and after about two hours the policewoman from the day before came to get me. I saw the face of my lawyer, a close friend of Nirosh's; he had an expression that I was unable to decipher. I asked him what was happening and he told me that, unfortunately, the Sri Lankan bank had blocked my accounts due to a misunderstanding with Italy. Unfortunately, in the meantime, we had run into a kind of local mafioso and, in any event, the law provided that I should stay in prison until the cheque was honoured. Among other things, 30 days had now passed and the court in Galle had opened my case.

I asked the lawyer to contact Mars. The account was blocked, but a money transfer would allow the bank to pay that person. Very simple on paper. The technical time to perform the operation in Italy would only take a few days.

"What will happen in the meantime?"

The lawyer shrugged: I would need to stay there "indefinitely, until the case was resolved"; translated into Sri Lanka, it meant very little. The lawyer had to leave and his next visit would be the following week.

I couldn't stay in there! I had to work, look after my dogs... what was I doing in a prison in the south of Sri Lanka? Who knows how Nande must have felt when he was deported there after Eileen's death and charged with crimes he didn't commit. How long had he stayed in there?

The lawyer expected to resolve the issue in a month. *A month?* And there I was, thinking I'd be staying only one night!

I went back to Nede, who after receiving the news looked at me with a compassionate air and offered me a cigarette. She gave me some advice on how to get by during those days. She told me that the biggest problems were the lice and infections: it turned out to be harder than expected. The camp bed was putrid, unfortunately I was already used to the cockroaches, but there were huge spiders that crawled all over your body at night that I couldn't help thinking about and there were lice everywhere.

Washing was the hardest task because there were no towels and sometimes I remained wet all night; it soon made me feel even more filthy.

By now, I hated *rice and curry*: that metal tray filled with lentils and red and very spicy broth made me gag.

I thought about Nande a lot during those days, so I asked the guard if there was still someone who had worked there since 1960 and he told me that maybe the old guardian might know something. The next morning, the policewoman came to me accompanied by the old man. The guardian said that he had met Nande Wijesinghe, who had been there for seven years, after which the court in Galle had made him guardian of the town's cinnamon plantation, given his previous positions in the field of botany. It was a kind of pre-trial detention and he wasn't allowed to leave Boussa. The old man, who didn't even introduce himself, also knew me and had seen me wandering around the area several times.

I resisted as best I could, during those days, battling nausea, the feeling of dirt and boredom. They came to get me on 20 February: Sam and Nirosh had found a relatively quick way to get me out of there, getting the money from loan sharks by using our old tuk-tuk as collateral. They had managed to calm down the man who had lodged a complaint against me for a while... I could leave if I promised to pay off my debt as soon as the money arrived from Italy.

It was time to say goodbye: it hadn't been that long, but it's amazing how quickly people adapt to any situation, so much so that they become part of it in no time.

I would be living not far from there, but I would look at that place differently from now onwards, a place which I only used to see from the perimeter wall as I passed by on my walks.

I promised that I would come back often to bring the other inmates all the basic necessities and, if possible, a little human warmth. I said goodbye to the guards, to whom I promised a few bottles of Arak.

Sampatha hugged me with tears in her eyes and I promised her that I would speak to my lawyer about her case. Nede was sitting smoking as usual and she didn't even get up to say goodbye, even though I caught a glimpse of complicity in her gaze. I told her to come and visit me when she got out but, in my heart, I knew it was probably more likely that I would be visiting her every week.

A survey conducted by non-governmental organisations revealed that the Sri Lankan judicial and prison system often perpetrates human rights violations against women and I was well aware of that, also given Sampatha's case. In particular, it was found that 50% of women in prison hadn't committed crimes, as such, but had been sentenced to imprisonment for not being able to pay a debt or a fine.

The problem was that once in prison, women are subjected to often inhumane treatment, eating food riddled with worms, sleeping without a bed or pillow, and sharing toilets with many other inmates. Furthermore, access to these services was forbidden after half past five in the afternoon, so the women were forced to use buckets that were kept in the cells. You can easily imagine the hygienic conditions the inmates were forced to live in.

Yet, I experienced a strange feeling, I was almost sad to leave them, in spite of that hell. When I walked through the gate, I realised that nothing is more important than freedom.

We often don't realise that we are free, but that day I thought of the thousands of people who live segregated, restricted, painful lives. Not necessarily in prison, but somehow forced to submit to something that doesn't allow them to be free. I had seen many, around the world, but I didn't yet know and couldn't understand.

Indian widows, who are locked up in Ashrams for life after the death of their master husbands, for example; or Kayan women, called "giraffe women", who sought shelter in Thailand, refugees from Myanmar and practically locked up in open-air zoos. I thought of those who didn't have the freedom to live the life they would have wanted due to political problems or racial impositions and I also thought of Nande and Eileen, who lived in an era of racial prejudices and ethnic differences, where wealthy settlers had often restricted and humiliated those they had subjugated.

I had always loved life very much, but that day I savoured freedom like I had never done so before and I thought that, despite everything, that experience hadn't managed to make me hate that strange country. It was just another new experience and, once again, I thought that everything happens for a reason.

CHAPTER 14

Once I was free again, I immersed myself in my work: the container from Bali would arrive soon, it was almost time.

I returned to Wirdana and sat down by the lake to look at my masterpiece; the fireflies were returning to light up the darkness.

After months of bulldozers and excavations, the birds had reappeared to build their nests in the garden, there were more than ten peacocks and the herons began stopping over for winter during their migration. I had put some fish in the pond, carp and small goldfish: I stopped to look at them for hours and I noticed that they all lived together except a large fish that had been saved from the lake during the excavations that attacked any of the others who drew close. The boys had said it would be difficult to keep it in there, so I checked every day to make sure he hadn't killed any of the other tenants in the pond. His fighting temperament probably wasn't suited to that situation!

The next morning, I took a closer look and found the answer: dozens of tiny fish had been born around the grey fish. It was a mother who was defending her little ones! She alternated between moments in which she kept them all in her mouth to protect them and moments in which she taught them to move around their new territory.

It had made me all warm inside and once the reason for her aggression was clear, I decided to keep her. I had also seen birds fighting with all their might to protect young ones who were learning to fly from predators.

Various species of birds had come to the garden: kingfishers, herons, small parrots in various colours and other small yellow and orange birds whose name I didn't know.

In the evening, the meadow filled with hares and squirrels everywhere; the fireflies had returned more numerous than before, a group of monkeys had settled on the highest palms and moved around by jumping from tree to tree. A few shiny, pitch black buffaloes grazed quietly and two cute lizards appeared from time to time for a quick hello.

The lake was filled with small frogs that croaked on hot days, making a sound that was similar to the shouting of children. My dogs had marked their territory and ran around happily.

I saw it as a little corner of paradise, where animals had found their habitat, just like me. In addition, my neighbours often brought me small gifts, delicious holiday treats or large freshly picked coconuts, wild rice or succulent papayas.

I'd got into the habit of walking around the village, often early in the morning, and I'd met several people in the surrounding area: the old woman from the fruit shop, the women who accompanied the children to school and the old man who brought fish to the village on his bike every day.

I often stopped to exchange a few words with the guardian of the small level crossing and waited with the women of the village for the return of the fishermen. I often went to the nearby school to speak a little English with the little schoolchildren in their white uniforms.

That, as I understood almost immediately, was the most beautiful and carefree time for those children, one of the most peaceful moments of their life, which would later become anything but simple.

CHAPTER 15

Summer came and I decided to take some time off and go to Trinco (as the Sinhalese like to call Trincomalee). I would take advantage of summer on the east coast to continue my research.

I got on an old bus that crossed the island, skirting the easternmost part and passing through Matata, Tangalle and Yala park, climbing along the wild coastline. I stopped in a little spot, a bay with crystal clear waters renowned for surfing: Arugam Bay, a small village enlivened by Australian surfers and modest guest houses, a magical place, far from everywhere and away from the beaten track, beaches with dunes and crocodiles, scattered with small cemeteries by the sea and water buffalo farms.

Then, I continued further north, through deserted towns and empty plantations, wild elephant territory, hundreds of miles of roads strewn with rubber trees.

We got to Trinco the following afternoon; I couldn't wait to stretch my legs a little, but first I took a room at a small guest house by the sea. Trinco is an incredible place: there are immaculate beaches and a pristine sea, even if military outposts are still omnipresent behind that paradise. It gave me the impression of a people who were still unable to believe that the war was truly over. Black crows circled the beaches like sentries, a few back packers were sprawled on the sand, smoking marihuana while the reminiscences of bloody battles and cruel genocides still filled the air.

Little or nothing is known about the Tamil war in Europe. The foundations for the civil war were laid when the Tamils, who were subjected to severe discrimination, organised themselves into a party, the Tamil Tigers, a name that made them seem ferocious, but which, at the beginning, merely reflected proud souls who wanted to regain their dignity. They created an independent state in the north, Tamil Eeelam, populated by descendants of the first deportees of the British who had never found peace.

However, during the seventies, what began as a non-violent struggle for the creation of a Tamil State became a justification for a violent rebellion by the Tigers, who also used "kamikaze" women, who at the time weren't called that; over the years, the Sinhalese army and the Tamil group alternated being in control of the north-eastern region and various attempts were made to make peace, none of which were successful.

At its peak in 2000, the Tigers controlled two-thirds of the territories of Sri Lanka's eastern and northern provinces. Over the years, the conflict and civil war resulted in more than 70,000 Tamil and Sinhalese, civilian and soldier, casualties. Only in 2006 were the Tamils isolated by the army from Colombo, which launched a violent offensive of which very little is known even now and was only officially declared in 2009. The groups of human rights activists vehemently criticised the government's "victory", partly due to the treatment meted out to Tamil civilians, who were locked up in de facto concentration camps.

To the eyes of the rest of the world, the country was transformed into a media black hole from which only orphans, refugees and corpses emerged. Even now, the government tries to hide what actually happened in one of the bloodiest wars in recent decades. After all, Sri Lanka still faces a delicate and difficult balancing act that will determine the future of the island.

There are stories of young soldiers who were unable to comprehend the decisions taken by their fathers, a war that flared up in the streets with unjustified violence: houses were set on fire, land was destroyed, lives were lost. However, there were also stories of friendships: after all, Tamils and Sinhalese lived close together in the same territory, often receiving and giving hospitality to each other, forming bonds and creating improbable love stories... just because someone had decided that they had to be enemies.

However, at that moment, that war seemed distant, impossible to imagine had it not been for the presence of soldiers everywhere. I stopped for a beer on the beach: what I knew and had to look for was a single name, Gayan Wijesinghe or something similar. He was a soldier and the last, sad news we had of him had reached Tulsie from here. I didn't know anything else. Was I a madwoman because I kept looking for information regarding men who were probably long dead?

I didn't know where to start and perhaps not even what I wanted to achieve. Perhaps I'd find news of Nande's son? What for? Nothing, I just seemed to *owe it to him*.

I met a kind boy called Emil on the white beach in Nilweli and, speaking to him, I learnt that the Trinco military base was located near the large natural harbour in the old Portuguese fort. All the soldiers had been there, sooner or later, because it was the largest outpost of the Sinhalese army before entering Tamil territory and the last fierce battles had been fought there. I knew it was like looking for a needle in a haystack, but I had to try.

Emil offered to accompany me to the base, he was enterprising and sharp and his father had also been killed during the civil war.

We arrived at around noon. He told me that it would take 1000 rupees to bribe the keepers of the archive and told me to wait there. After half an hour, he returned smiling and confirmed that we could take a look at the archives. We entered the Trincomalee naval base with just a name and a date; 1982. I felt like laughing, I really must have been mad! I was looking for the dead son of a ghost that I had practically fallen in love with and hadn't even known!

After Emil's mediation, I realised once more that everything was bought there. Life, death, information and help. Everything has a price. That 1000 rupees actually served to buy us access to the registers.

We leafed through the registers of 1982 for hours, but the infernal heat and fatigue made me wilt. I decided to stop that absurd treasure hunt, it had been more than enough for one day; we would be back the next morning.

I stayed on the beach with Emil that evening and he told me his story. He was one of the so-called "beach boys", youngsters who leave their homes to find work on the tourist beaches in some bar or guest house, free themselves from their constraints, often grow their hair, dress in a European-style and dream of Europe. They listen to Western music and the stories told by tourists, hoping gain new knowledge that makes them feel free. They forget their traditions, their culture and live as if there was no tomorrow. Only the here and now and a single goal: get to the West to change their lives.

There are thousands of them, here as in all tourist destinations throughout the world. Often they just want to talk, they view a European friend as an open door towards their dreams. I don't think they love their country less than others, but they often feel trapped in a vice of constraints from which they want to break free. How can you blame them?

Emil told me about a Danish girlfriend of his, who had gone there on vacation two years earlier. He proudly showed me a photo of a pale girl that he had never seen again, but who had promised to take him to Europe one day. I knew it wasn't true, and so did Emil, deep down, but he kept hoping that she would return one day.

He was very endearing as he told me about his great love; he proudly stated that he would never have an arranged marriage and that he would never accept his family's rules.

"I'm free to choose!", he said, as he'd written on the side of his scooter, borrowing an old phrase from Bob Marley.

He worked as a bartender in a small beach bar that resembled the one on Baradise beach. It was in the same style with cook's wood, chains of shells hanging everywhere and beautiful music that perhaps some young tourist had left him. The walls were adorned with posters of Che Guevara, Jack Sparrow and Bob Marley, the idols of that generation of young Sinhalese. It was a nice, relaxing place. Being on the east coast, you couldn't watch the sunset, but the moon was spectacular in the evening: it looked so large that when it was reflected in the sea it lit everything up almost as if it were day.

It was late and exhausting research awaited us the next day, so I said goodbye and we arranged to meet the following day.

When we returned to the base the next morning, the keeper had changed and the person who had taken our 1000 rupees had disappeared; they told Emil that I wasn't welcome and that I had to leave. A woman, worse still a European one, was undoubtedly not popular at a military base in a country with such a macho heritage.

I waited at the exit of the fort and lay down in the shade of a large tree, under which a statue of the fallen was erected; the garden was full of giant-horned deer grazing freely. It was surreal: deer a few steps from the sea! I was exhausted from the heat and didn't even know how long I would have to wait, so I dozed off.

Upon awakening, I looked at the statue above me and I realised that there was a long list of war dead. My heart started beating fast: I had long since started believing in coincidences and how things don't happen by accident. I started scrolling through the names in an endless list... until I reached w and then Wijesinghe. There were dozens of them, but then...

Gayan Welivita Dewasatta Wijesinghe! Thank god the name of the father always appears in their descendants' names. Year of death 1983: so, the year I was looking for was wrong, perhaps Tulsie was confused.

I immediately called Emil, who was inside the base, to give him the news and tell him where and what to look for.

A few soldiers were playing cricket in the courtyard and the sun filtered through the columns of the colonial buildings that once housed barracks and garrisons. While I was waiting for Emil, I stopped for a Chai in a small bar in the fort and couldn't stop thinking about the coincidences that had brought me there. To the little colonial house, to the diary, to the relationships between my life and that of Nande, Eileen, Watawala, Tulsie... why had I got myself involved in that absurd story?

Immersed in my thoughts, I saw Emil running out of the base holding some papers. He'd found something, he was hardly able to control his excitement, like he had found a long-lost relative.

Those papers contained everything about Gayan Wijesinghe, the day of his recruitment, awards, imprisonment and the date of his death, which occurred on 1 May 1983. Executed. A shiver ran down my back, what did it mean that he had been executed? Not fallen in battle? The most incredible thing was that there was even an address where he had lived in his war years.

It was an address on an island north of Trinco near Jaffna, the scene of the last battles of the civil war and the last Tamil bulwark; Emil knew that name, a place in the wilderness where they probably didn't even know that the war was actually over. It was the feeling I had after I had just arrived in the north of the country: those soldiers were still there to watch over the territory as if the war had never ended or, rather, as if they were incredulous and still didn't believe it. They still patrolled the streets, the fields, as if at any moment a Tamil guerrilla might still pop up somewhere, as if someone could still appear suddenly and attack them from the bush.

The address or, rather, the name of the island was Delft.

The coastal road led to a village two hours from Trinco, an agglomeration of houses, farmers and buffalo herders. From there, we would get to the island.

Neduntheevu in Tamil, but Delft for everyone else, is a flat island surrounded by shallow, turquoise waters and beaches of sand and coral blocks. It's home to a small population of Tamils who fled here during the war. The ramshackle boats arrive here in the morning and leave in the late afternoon. Outsiders never sleep on the island.

The junker used to reach the island of Delft was a public ferry, operated by the Sri Lankan government; it didn't have particularly comfortable seats and could get quite humid on board. The other, noisy passengers seemed to ignore the giant waves crashing on the old junker, which tossed from side to side, taking on water at each powerful jolt.

We had also loaded Emil's scooter, others had loaded engines, turbines, some even parts of houses! The journey lasted more than an hour in those conditions, then the dark water slowly began to become transparent and shades of turquoise that I had only seen in the most beautiful tropical seas lit up.

Finally, a turquoise postcard port appeared on the horizon, together with some equally turquoise fishing boats moored neatly in that picturesque painting.

A "please, protect nature" sign welcomed those who landed on the island, as if the island wanted to protect itself, knowing that it was terribly fragile.

When we arrived at the small village, most of the old historic buildings we saw were dilapidated. Barracks, stables and perhaps what must have been an aviary. Indeed, during the Portuguese era, pigeons were the only way of communicating.

The lack of local tourists probably wasn't motivation enough to look after the beaches, which were a bit dirty, but the sea was beautiful. On the way to the beach, you could also admire the fences of the houses built entirely of coral. A intertwining cluster of brain corals and lace held together only by gravity.

Travelling across the wasteland on our motorbike, we met massive herds of beautiful, majestic wild horses in a vast meadow. It's believed that they were introduced to the island by colonisers who bred horses here for taming. Beautiful and shy, they allowed us to approach and then turned abruptly and galloped away, their manes blown by the wind that whips the west of the island incessantly.

I was delighted by that unknown splendour: how could such a wonderful place remain hidden from the world, why did no one talk about it and why had no one thought of going there? Far less beautiful places had become popular tourist destinations even here in Sri Lanka. Not even Emil knew about this place or, rather, he had heard of it, but had never been here.

We forgot why we were there for a while and stopped at one of the beaches on the east of the small island. Like two children, we dived into the crystalline waters. The water was warm, as it is everywhere in the Indian Ocean, the beach was covered with wonderful shells and the sea was teeming with multicoloured fish. We were alone, not a soul in sight: those immaculate beaches weren't used by anyone, it was incredible that so much beauty was left uninhabited.

I began to fantasise and, in my head, I had already designed a small coral house with large windows overlooking the sea, where I could lose myself on my days of total relaxation sometime in the future.

We left again on Emil's scooter and close to sunset we arrived at a hill by the sea on the side of the island that turns towards India, whipped by the winds where the Queen's Tower was located, perhaps one of the most fascinating remains left by the Dutch. Although simple in architectural terms, it was perhaps one of the most fascinating lighthouses in the Indian Ocean. A fire was lit at the base of the tower and the light carried up through the tunnel becomes a beacon for ships on dark and stormy nights.

From that height, we saw our boat leaving the small port without us.

We were so excited that we'd forgotten the time for the return journey.

We thought it wasn't such a bad thing and that we would find a sheltered place to spend the night on the island and the next morning we'd get to the house where we might find news of Gayan, even if in our hearts we were not at all sure.

We got to a small building built completely of coral near the island's post office: it was simple, but oddly clean and would be just fine for the night.

We lit a fire in the small courtyard, we had bananas, some biscuits and water: we had everything we needed for the night. Emil was very protective of me and had taken the role of man of the house.

Our fire soon attracted the attention of some people from the village, but no one had yet dared to approach.

As we were chatting excitedly about what we were going to do the next day, at a certain point, a tall young man with very delicate features approached. His name was Dinusha, he immediately started talking to Emil in Tamil and only after a long conversation with him did he speak to me; he spoke English perfectly and I asked him what he was doing on that remote island. Behind him appeared the small figure of a boy who must have been about 25 years old. Emil nodded affirmatively to the boy, who look intimidated as he approached: his name was Isuru.

They had a bottle of arak and, after a few too many sips, they felt free to tell me their story.

They had always loved each other, but in order to have their love story, they had decided to leave their village near Jaffna and move there, to that remote place swept by the wind, where no one would find them. Once again, I had to refrain from saying what I wanted and listened in silence.

Dinusha told me that, like him, many people had been subjected to humiliating body searches that supposedly to checked the homosexuality of a person by looking at their most intimate parts: it still happened, there, in a country notorious for its harsh laws against what, in the penal code, is defined as "carnal relations against the order of nature" and "obscene acts between people".

I thought that, in the twenty-first century, no one should be arrested, much less tortured or subjected to sexual violence based on suspicions related to their sexual orientation.

In that year alone, for example, nine men were placed under arrest on charges of having committed acts contrary to the law and morals, as revealed by an account released by the Sri Lankan police force, which was careful not to mention the vast number of intimidations and violent acts to which those arrested were subjected. In some cases, the harassment of the officers who arrested those poor people had even culminated in rape.

Their story shocked me. I could only say that now they could rest easy and no longer worry about all the hurt they had been subjected to.

The following morning, we set off on Emil's motorbike, who had come to see himself as something of a hero, and travelled through the most desolate area of Sri Lanka; at least, that's what it looked like to me.

There were a handful of tourists and foreigners in general. The village or, rather, the few scattered houses, made Watawala look like a metropolis.

I knew full well that the date was 35 years ago and that we probably wouldn't find anything, but I couldn't stop now.

The small village they had told us about was made of mud and coral houses, as was traditional, scattered on a large clearing. Once again, I thought how mad I must be. We arrived at our destination in the evening and, incredibly, found the very house that had belonged to Gayan. It was the right address. In the doorway, an old man who was sitting and chewing betel frowned at us.

There were only old people and children on the island: the middle generation had practically disappeared due to the war, as I had also seen in Cambodia. Emil approached the man and they began to speak in Sinhala.

They talked for more than an hour, as I had often seen: lots of words, very long and excited discussions to say only a few concepts, during which they offered me tea heated on a wood fire. Emil looked sad at the end of the conversation, as if he had been told that someone in his family had died. He sat down next to me and told me what speaking to the old man had revealed.

He told me that Gayan had married a Tamil woman for love, which had already caused him a lot of trouble with the army. He told me that she had been killed a few years later by an army patrol.

They had discovered that Gayan had also helped her to hide some Tamil rebels and that was why he'd been executed, which is what the law required as a punishment for traitors.

However, there was more: they had had a child and the little one, with no one to care for him, was added to the endless list of little war orphans who had been given up for adoption, an endless list of little ones saved by volunteers and given up for adoption to different parts of the world.

The only thing known about the little one was that his name was Channa.

Therefore, he was somewhere far away, somewhere in the world, probably in Europe.

I had truly done everything I could: I had discovered what had happened to Nande's son and I had even discovered that he had a grandson named Channa: somewhere, a piece of Nande still lived! His life had been worth something and

I hoped that the child, now a grown man, had managed to redeem his life and that he had had an opportunity, perhaps, to live a happy family life. Perhaps even had the chance to study, who knows...

The next morning, as we left Delft, I had the strange feeling that it would be difficult to go back there, I hoped that as few people as possible would find out how beautiful it was, that no one would deface it. As we departed on the old junker of the sea and the turquoise waters turned gloomy once more, an infinite sadness came over me as I thought about Gayan and his Tamil bride, who had taken refuge here to escape a world of persecution, like the two boys had done, but had not been lucky. Only little Channa had somehow managed to save himself, but who knows where he was now! I turned once again to watch Delft move further away: I saw it disappear and got the feeling that it was sinking into the ocean.

Only years later did I learn something terrible about the fate of that wonderful island, which unfortunately would be just one of the countless disasters that would scar my Ceylon.

Sri Lanka sold three islands in the North Sea over the years that followed, including the island of Delft, the largest island in Sri Lanka. They were sold to China for three energy projects;

although declared renewable energy projects, many believe China will use them as bases for nuclear energy projects.

Unfortunately, the national debt of this fragile country would soon lead it to having to repay the Chinese giant, not with money, but with pieces of the country itself.

We went back to Trinco flying on the motorbike and skirting the turquoise sea.

We spent the last evening on the beach and Emil told his friends about our great adventure: romanticising the story to the other boys made him feel like a hero for a moment, before returning to his everyday life and his dreams.

The next morning, I said goodbye to Emil and his desire to live in Europe; I told him that one day I would do anything I could to help him, one way or another, to fulfil his dream.

I got on the express bus to Galle, while Emil followed me on his scooter, his long hair blowing in the wind. He got smaller and smaller, then disappeared and I fell asleep thinking about Delft, that wonderful place we'd discovered by accident. I thought about how many places like that there had to be, places that needed to be protected like jewels in such a precarious world, where giants like India and China were ready to destroy helpless jewels.

CHAPTER 16

Staying there, the feeling I had had for a long time was that of being at home.

The works at Wirdana were almost finished and it was time to move there, I had found my staff, willing youngsters who would soon become my "team".

The first to arrive was Santhe, a frail, delicate little man who didn't speak a word of English, but who worked like a machine, never getting tired; every now and then I caught him singing and whistling and it filled me with cheer.

Then came Sumudu. A former soldier with a proud, bold air. He knew how to do everything and moved confidently. He owned a black tuk-tuk that he had bought with his life's savings and on which there was an inscription that summarised his nature: "Never underestimate the little common man". It sounded like a perfect slogan for him.

Then there was Heranga, he came from what must have been one of the poorest families in the village; they still lived in a mud hut, but he had a lot of experience and moved like a prince. Sometimes, his fairness and education almost managed to embarrass me.

My chef had also arrived, a little round man who had worked in Dubai for a number of years, he knew how to prepare sublime dishes that we came up with together, creating our menu with products from the vegetable garden.

I had asked Nirosh to stay and work with me and he hadn't hesitated to leave his job to help me: his experience and his education were now indispensable to me.

They'd become my family and I could no longer do without them.

Wirdana was wonderful. Over time, I had placed large light-coloured sofas around the small, breezy lake, the bedrooms were spacious and now furnished with beds topped with large mosquito nets. The usual, fabulous light, which had made me fall in love with the place, filtered through from the imposing windows. The large saltwater pool dominated the flower garden and the lake sparkled in the sun. My lotus flowers had already grown.

The garden was even greener after the rainy season, Nande's trees were lush and the mangoes ripe, it was all as I had dreamt it would be and I was serene. I had given meaning to my life and to Nande's existence, who must have been a wonderful man and who, like many others, had paid the price for a difficult life.

In this country, where no one gives you anything, we had practically lived three intense years together, side by side: he had unknowingly given me so much and I hoped I had repaid what I owed him, albeit only through my attempts to reconstruct his story.

Perhaps now he could rest a little more in peace and a part of him still lived in Wirdana.

Everything I had built was also thanks to him and, had it not been for his advice on insect bites and magical herbs, I would probably have been dead. I told myself that everything I would experience from then on would also be for him.

Wirdana was now ready for my guests; I didn't know how it would turn out, but, in my heart, I knew I was making a small contribution to help that fantastic country rise from the ashes. Indeed, a part of the world would discover these places thanks a little to me.

I knew that now my home was there, among the palm trees and the colours of that land, among the fantastic people of Sri Lanka from whom I still had so much to learn.

It was just the beginning of my adventure.
There, in Wirdana, I was happy again.

It had been almost a year since I had moved to Wirdana; my days went by calmly, I had finally found some peace. Of course, I always had a lot to do, but I liked to wake up at dawn to go to the fish market, where I chose freshly caught jewels. I liked to go and buy fruit and the first fruits that changed with the seasons, I went to the fort and walked the streets to look for more items to complete Wirdana. Oils and herbs in Ayurvedic shops or scented incense for the spa.

In the evenings, I often had a drink at the Baradise and spent the evenings laughing and joking with the Rasta boys who sang and played, or I would see Karla and together we would take long walks or eat at some restaurant in the fort.

Many friends had come to visit me from Italy and Bali and many more would soon come; Mars had also come back and I saw he was truly happy to see what I had done, subconsciously complicit in my adventure. I thought that, in any case, perhaps I would never have had the courage to start all of this without him.

I also liked to stop and chat with my guests: lots of different stories from every corner of the world. Norwegians, Australians, Barein Arabs or Argentines, curious people who were often discovering this country for the first time. They asked a lot of questions and I enjoyed telling them my story.

That peace also allowed me to cultivate my spiritual side. I wasn't a Buddhist, yet every day I got into the habit of going to the temple. Let's say that I had got to know many religions closely and I had often found myself agreeing with various doctrines. I had shared Jain ceremonies and tried to understand respect for the smallest forms of life, I had chanted mantras, attended Hindu cremations, learnt not to be afraid of earthly death, read about animist religions, hugged trees and learnt to acknowledge the sanctity of all living forms.

However, I had long realised that physical places were nothing, that doctrines were merely a way to get to something else and that prayers were only a means.

I often felt my spiritual side emerge in surprising moments and I found peace in different places, where I never thought I'd find it.

I enjoyed going to the small temple close to home to relax, it gave me a feeling of peace, like no other place. It was very old, built on giant rocks that seem to fly, like most of the holy places in Sri Lanka. In parts of the country, I had often seen temples built near giant rocks that seemed to fly and hover lightly against gravity and I realised that all the sacred places I had visited in Sri Lanka were somehow connected. Sigirya itself, considered the eighth wonder of the world, was an immense rock of hardened magma that rose from nothing to a height of 1968 feet; palaces and monasteries had been built on its peak, entire civilisations lived on the top of the lion's rock and many legends and mysteries, still unsolved today, add to the mystery of this unique place.

However, Sigirya was certainly not the only place shrouded in the mystery of giant rocks: Buduruwagala and its seven immense Buddha statues carved into a solitary rock in the middle of the jungle, illuminated by the sun's rays through the bush, was a magical place of peace and serenity.

All those places had rock carvings called Sellipi in Singhala in common, carvings which no one has ever been able to decipher.

All kinds of legends were told about these places, there was talk of aliens and doorways to other dimensions. I don't have the means to comment, let alone validate these superstitions, but what I can say with certainty is that every time I drew close to or entered those places, something special happened to me and I felt overwhelmed by incredible sensations.

"My" temple was a landmark for the village, monks studied there and the "head" monk was the most revered person. You had to take off your shoes, as was the case in many sacred places on the planet, and signs urged silence and respect.

The mantras had already begun that morning and a young couple was praying together, perhaps to prepare for an upcoming wedding. A young monk was teaching mantras to a small group of attentive children in their white uniforms, while a woman lit puja and arranged flowers and offerings. The light was still dim and there was an enchanted atmosphere, as if suspended in time.

A small staircase preceded by a semi-circular moonstone led to a ravine in the suspended rocks: you entered a kind of cave where a ray of light illuminated the stone statue of a Buddha.

That day, like every day, I took some incense to light them and went to the brazier, as I had done every morning a thousand times, but after a few seconds I felt a presence behind me.

I saw a hand with long fingers that helped me to light the fire: I turned slowly and saw a tall, smiling man behind me in the dim light.

A pair of deep eyes, thick eyebrows and the same mouth, the same proud air that I had seen so many times in that photograph and in my mind: Nande!!

It couldn't be him! I must have really gone mad, so I turned around a second time, thinking that the figure would disappear, but he was still there.

I almost ran out into the sunlight and sat down by the great sacred tree that overlooks all the temples with my heart in my mouth. I hoped the figure would disappear into thin air, but instead I saw him come out of the cave and come towards me with a sweet smile.

"Are you Wirdana madam?", he asked me in English. Immediately afterwards he said, "I'm Channa... I've been looking for you for some time!"

CHAPTER 17

It was him, Nande's grandson, a carbon copy of his grandfather.

In a single instant, everything I had ever imagined became real.

Sometimes, there we encounter people who are totally unknown to us, in whom we are interested from the very first glance. Suddenly, unexpectedly, even before a single word has been spoken.

I already knew that those who are worth loving are those who make you different and new, those who manage to accompany you on your new journey, managing to keep you alive in a jungle you know nothing about, where you would die were it not for them. They accompany you with their gestures, their words and teach you the steps and, against all odds, you manage to follow them.

We fell madly in love, despite our differences, our distances, despite the obstacles and barriers.

When your heartbeat exceeds the shadows of the past, love can triumph over destiny. The most important encounters are already arranged by our souls, even before our bodies see each other. Of course, people happen *per chance* in our lives, but never *by chance*.

Sometimes, they make us fly high, other times they make us crash into the ground, teaching us pain; giving us everything, taking everything away, leaving us alone or in company, but despite everything we love them and we're willing to throw ourselves back into the waves each time, convinced we know how to swim.

It's strange that in the West we think of relationships in terms of needs and rights... if a person doesn't give us what we're looking for, we often think that the right thing to do is leave them, but there love is seen as a supernatural force, which can undoubtedly harm ordinary things, such as goals or needs, but which sooner or later becomes something that goes beyond everything. I found it wonderful to get lost in this new way of experiencing love and I felt like I had never done so before.

From that moment on, we were as one, we spent days exploring each other and exploring that new life, trying to put together the pieces that had brought us here, savouring that world together, seeing it with new eyes.

I wanted to know everything about his story, even though it was as if we had always known one another: I almost knew more about his life than he did, but together we could fill those gaps that weighed heavily on his past. As I already knew, he was one of the war orphans, children who are now almost 40 years old, some even younger, but who in the 1980s were just babies when they were snatched from their mothers' arms. They often lost their identities forever and were handed over to European families for adoption, leaving behind a past that was difficult to recover.

He told me that a few years earlier he had accidentally seen a Dutch documentary that shed light on the big business of illegal adoptions in Sri Lanka. In the midst of the civil war, over eleven thousand newborn babies from the Asian country had been handed over to European families with false documents on both sides. Many of them were even born on so-called farms: "baby factories", where pregnant women lived in semi-incarceration and, after giving birth, had their children sold to the West.

The business presumably involved influential people, who helped falsify documents: birth certificates, children's names and the identities of their biological parents. The latter, however, were often unaware of what had happened. They were told that their children had died, when in fact they had been sold abroad.

Several pages were set up on Facebook to help children adopted in Sri Lanka to trace their origins and biological mothers to track down their children, who had disappeared into thin air. Even the Sri Lankan Ministry of Health stated at the time that it would create a database to facilitate the searches. This is what happened to Channa.

His parents, however, were dead; the story had touched him profoundly and since then the call of his past had nevertheless been very strong.

"What made you want to come back after so many years?", I asked him. In my heart, I already knew there was something more, but Channa hesitated.

He had lived in Holland in an adopted family who adored him, then he studied medicine and graduated and then practiced the profession, specialising in natural medicine. Ayurveda, coincidentally, but something had prompted him to return to work there and put into practice what he had and would have learned, like his grandfather; at the very same time as I was digging into his past.

It couldn't have been a coincidence.

We spoke about Nande for a long time, I told him the whole incredible story and as I had imagined, I knew more about his grandfather than he had learned from his contacts; he told me that at the end of his search, he had learned that an Italian woman had bought his grandfather's land and that was how he had found me.

Destiny sometimes helps us more than we can imagine.

It was only after a few days that he began to talk to me about something he owned, the only object that his mother had put in the cradle with him before she died and he was taken away. That object had always stayed with him throughout his life in Europe and discovering the meaning of the object soon became his raison d'etre.

He showed me something that looked like a dark parcel wrapped in string, but it was much more than that. He explained that it was a "leaf of destiny" that could reveal what he was looking for, but the complete explanation would only come to light if he, or rather we, went to the city of Tanjore, in the south of the Indian state of Tamil Nadu, not far from the coasts of Ceylon, in the ancient Mahal Saravasti library, which holds the secrets of the most sought after and, at the same time, most feared treasure on earth: our destiny!

It's all written on dried palm leaves in an ancient language, Sanskrit, and it seems that they contain the past, present and future life of all those who are destined to come to that place to find out what the future holds. The leaves of destiny are not limited to a single people or nation, but the whole of humanity. It's said that anyone who is destined to know their destiny will find themselves in that place, at a precise moment in their lives, to know what the future holds for them... and after consulting their leaf, they will use it as a true guide for knowing themselves.

I was fascinated and it was like returning to my search for Nande's secrets: it wasn't over yet! How many things did that family still hide and how much more would I have been involved in it?

To reach the library, we had to go to the far north of the country, cross the Mannar peninsula and the Rama Strait before disembarking in the ghost town of Dhanushkodi. A little further north, in the land of the Indian Tamils, in Tanjiore, we would reach that place.

Without even having to be asked, I had already packed my bags.

I was ready to go with him, I was no longer alone; it was like travelling with Nande at my side, I was as excited and happy as I had ever been.

We disembarked in India, just off the coast of Sri Lanka, and reached the city of Dhanushkodi, whose name actually means "end of the arch", given the arched geographical position before the strait that separates India from Sri Lanka. It's full of unusual and, sadly, tragic anecdotes. In fact, the city has literally sunk into the sea.

Dhanushkodi was once a sacred site to which pilgrimages were made. However, nowadays only an empty city remains, in which everything has been swallowed up by water. It's basically a ghost town with a tragic recent history.

Indeed, the effects of the Rameswaram cyclone in 1964 had been tremendous. Since then, the city had disappeared below sea level, only to re-emerge quite unexpectedly during the tsunami in December 2004, when the sea around Dhanushkodi pulled back about 500 yards from the coast, revealing several remains of the city. However, life didn't flow back to those parts again.

I found it to be a lovely town with an unparalleled view of the blue waters, embraced by the confluence of the Indian Ocean and the Bay of Bengal. From there, a narrow strip of semi-submerged land jutted out, the so-called Adam's Bridge, which reaches the Sinhalese island of Mannar.

Modern industrialisation would like to exploit this narrow stretch of sea to build a bridge connecting India to the island of Ceylon in the near future, but the project for a bridge over the canal has been forcefully and fortunately opposed by environmentalists, but above all by religious groups of Buddhists, for years.

Thanks to recent satellite photos provided by NASA, Indian environmentalists became even more convinced of the veracity of their legends. The photos appear to reveal a curvature and a layout of the rocks that can only be explained by human intervention.

What's known for certain is that, in the past, it was normally travelled on foot and by means of transport until the connection was swept away by a terrible cyclone in 1480. If the bridge were artificial, it would be a more astounding piece of work than the pyramids or the Great Wall of China.

Having visiting Sigiriya and Anurathapura, I already knew about Sri Lanka's prosperous past, but my island never ceased to surprise me...

A little further north, we reached the city of Tajiore, where the library was located and where "the reader", the person who would decipher the leaf, previously contacted by Channa, was waiting for us on time.

Indeed, the reading took place by appointment and started with an opening ceremony of the archive, then the participants were fingerprinted: the thumb of the right hand for men and of the left hand for women, then the reader began to ask questions of the subject, in an almost hypnotic chant, about their life. They had to answer either "yes" or "no". The procedure was very long and could even last an entire day. As soon as the leaf was opened, the wonderful journey in their life began so that they could get to know, transform and improve it!

I was astounded and listened with amazement to everything they said to each other. It wasn't easy, especially in an age of scepticism like ours, to believe without having scientific evidence at hand, although there are many positive testimonies. It can seem very similar to predictions provided by horoscopes, which flood us with vague information every day, especially in Sri Lanka, but I'd never experienced the aura of mysticism and tradition that shrouded that place.

The reader closed his eyes and said to Channa, in Tamil, "Don't think of what the Oracle will tell you in terms of right or wrong. It's a guide. It merely has to help you find the way!

It only told you what you needed to hear, nothing more. Sooner or later, you'll understand that one thing is knowing the right path and another is taking it. If you find your leaf, it means that someone wanted you to know the true reason for the difficulties you face today, so that you might face them with less preoccupation. Remember, our life does not belong to us. From the womb to the grave, we are linked to events".

In that country, I h'd already understood that anything was possible if we began to look beyond our horizon, and I had proof of that once more.

The reader told us that something unexpected would happen soon, not just to us, but the entire world would soon be shocked by something huge... and that it would lead to a great awareness. Only those who had achieved awareness would be saved, only those who had renounced their earthly certainties would be able to endure what was about to happen.

He told Channa that he was one of them, because someone before him had opened the doors of the knowledge that had been handed down to him, but the real secret still had to be discovered: it was in the mountains of Ritigala and Channa's mission would be to unearth it and make it public in order to save many lives... yet, unfortunately, before that could happen many lives would be destroyed.

We left the library, but I didn't actually pay much attention to what the reader had said other than that we would have to continue this kind of endless treasure hunt; there wasn't much to say, except look at each other and think that we would soon be leaving for Ritigala.

CHAPTER 18

However, things didn't go as we had planned: Ritigala had to wait for various reasons and the events that followed changed our plans.

In April 2019, I'd been in Sri Lanka for four years; my love story with Channa had been flourishing for six months: he had opened a doctor's clinic and I was continuing my business at Wirdana, which was now shining on the island's tourism scene.

It was a short, peaceful period, perhaps the best in my life. We were happy and both of us had found part of what we had long sought. For me it was running away from my pain and arriving in Sri Lanka, for him it was revisiting the memories of his pain by returning there. However, it seemed that my happiness still needed to be tested and, unfortunately, soon the black clouds of the monsoon would not bring the rain!

On 21 April of that year, we woke up like every morning; Channa to go to the clinic and I took my dogs and went to Carla's place. It was Easter and I wanted to bring her something to celebrate together. I left early that morning, the sky was clear and the sea was calm, everything seemed perfect. I arrived at Carla's early, at that hour the volunteers were feeding the dogs and I, too, had brought some food that I had "stolen" from Wirdana's restaurant. We exchanged good wishes in an atmosphere of great complicity, as often happened when I went there. Shortly after, at around ten in the morning, I was on my way home when I noticed that there was something strange in the air: people on the street were agitated and were whispering as they looked at their mobile phones. I didn't understand what was happening, but I had the feeling that something terrible was happening, like when the news comes on and the latest, terrible news flashes hit the screen.

I just managed to get to Wirdana on time when the old guardian ran up to me and told me if I knew what had happened. I saw Channa, who was still in the street, talking agitatedly with the others and I immediately thought there might be more trouble with the police.

Unfortunately, that wasn't the case, it was much worse.

Some churches had been attacked by terrorists carrying bombs, but news flashes continued to arrive: three large hotels in the capital had been attacked. It was like seeing another 11 September.

The situation was by no means stable: explosions continued to take place in the country, the police were finding bombs, some of which were defused before they could do any damage. Shortly before, a bomb had gone off that they hadn't been able to defuse in time and three policemen had died.

News filtered through slowly, all social media was blocked immediately, while ISIS continued to disseminate messages via YouTube. Sri Lanka was under attack, peace was in grave danger and the risk that the exasperation of the population would explode into clashes was far from remote. We just had to stay very calm, even though it wasn't easy, because we felt like bombs were ready to go off everywhere. The media around the world started to spread terrible news and from there we couldn't figure out what was really going on. It was still night-time in Italy and no one was aware of what had happened, the Western world would soon wake up to the news of yet another terrible attack.

Many foreigners, generally tourists, were among the dead and wounded and many Christians, too, a church having been targeted during the Easter celebrations.

Quite frankly, the thought of a terrorist act had crossed my mind from the first moment I set foot in the country. I've always kept a keen eye on the phenomenon of terrorism. Looking at the facts, I thought it was practically impossible that such a complex and articulated terrorist operation could have completely escaped the attention of the security services... given the precariousness of the country's political system, someone should have had some warning!

News began to leak over the days that followed: ISIS had claimed responsibility for the attack, but it was clear that the self-styled Islamic State would have benefitted greatly by claiming responsibility for terrorist actions of this magnitude, even if it had had nothing to do with them. In Sri Lanka, at the time, it was well known that there was open war between the Presidency and the Government. I wondered if the attack really was due to Islamic terrorism or, rather, the bloody struggle between political and religious feuds involving powerful opposing groups in the country.

The theory that the massacre in Sri Lanka was just an episode in the confrontation between religions seemed quite fragile. Both Muslims and

Christians were, and still are, a minority in the country, which is actually dominated by classes and political forces of a nationalist and Buddhist majority.

There's bad blood between the two communities, undoubtedly, but at this point it was more likely that the real target of the attack was the local government. Indeed, the main target was the Sri Lankan tourist industry, three hotels having been hit and numerous foreigners murdered.

It was no secret that Sri Lanka was in a position of great strategic importance, which explained why China, India, Japan, the European powers and, surprise-surprise, the United States, which had recently obtained an unlimited docking permit at the port of Trincomalee, were very interested in maintaining their positions of power in the Indian Ocean, where Sri Lanka occupies a strategic position.

Once again, it was sad to see that certain civil wars or attacks were the result of unscrupulous imperialist strategies: a more or less independentist, separatist, minority group is financed with a vague ideological connotation, with the sole purpose of creating instability from within, which then allows for the sudden change of global geopolitical alliances, replacing one powerful group with another or forcing the country into chaos.

Sri Lanka is a fragile country, an ideal powder keg on which to carry out social experiments that can then be replicated on a global scale.

It's just an opinion of mine, but to date the real reasons for those attacks are still unclear or, perhaps, no one's really interested in making them known.

The incontrovertible truth was that everything was irremediably destroyed anyway. The blurred boundary between peace and war had been crossed and none of us knew when all this would be forgotten and when normality would return.

Nevertheless, we decided to stay, since leaving Sri Lanka would have been like betraying that people, as if to say: now that you're on the floor, I'm going to trample you and leave. Despite the curfews and continuing legacies, life would never be the same again.

Very soon, all the allegations regarding the attacks fell away, but there remained a country that had once again been mortally wounded and would find it increasingly difficult to recover. The biggest blow, as mentioned, had been inflicted on tourism and the tourist destination, considered the best in the world in 2019, had been annihilated by the fear of possible new attacks.

Obviously, no tourist would travel to such a precarious and unstable destination and, logically, Wirdana's business was also decimated. They were difficult months, in which everyone was terrified of both attacks and what would happen to the economy in the near future. Ambitions of tourism and the hope of a stable renaissance were clearly annihilated. A gloomy period followed, feuds between Buddhists and Muslims multiplied and often forced the Islamic population to hide and suffer attacks of all kinds.

Many of our friends were Muslims and the hatred they suffered at the time was truly unfair, senseless, although it certainly made sense to those who had planned everything that happened. They had destroyed an already fragile economy and planted even more hatred among the various ethnic groups and poor governance diverted attention from their own incompetence and encouraged the venting of public discontent towards a convenient scapegoat. Unfortunately, I wasn't the only one to be firmly convinced of it.

Meanwhile, my business at Wirdana, which had obviously been compromised, was transformed into a refuge for people in need; we spent the days trying to help those who needed it most, dozens of people came to the clinic and the resort every day to ask for help, people who had lost everything. They needed everything, sometimes they just sought comfort, other times food or

Ayurvedic concoctions to cure imaginary diseases just to be with someone for a while.

With tourism dead, a chain of events was triggered in which thousands of people lost their jobs and, as if that were not enough, everything that was imported became inaccessible and prices immediately skyrocketed. The poor were even poorer, if that were possible, and people no longer had faith in anything or anyone. Many hotels had to lay off thousands of people who had got a steady job through sheer hard work.

With the tourism industry virtually annihilated, the country fell into an abyss that it had slowly tried to avoid for years.

The vain attempts to tell the world that Sri Lanka was still a safe country proved in vain: the island once again plunged into a black hole and the world turned its head away.

CHAPTER 19

After a few months, around October of that year, we tried to use the time as best we could by continuing our research. In the meantime, Channa had studied everything he could about Nande, gathering everything he could find from the information in the diaries, in Ayurvedic texts and in the therapeutic instructions left by his grandfather. An important piece was still missing that we couldn't leave incomplete, so we decided to leave for Ritigala to get away from everything a little and be together alone for a while.

Ritigala is located in the east of Sri Lanka in the land of the Vedda, the ruins of the most fascinating monastery in Sri Lanka, engulfed by the jungle. It's in a context that's vaguely reminiscent of Angkor Wat. It's said that miraculous medicinal herbs grow there, which monks and natives used to heal wounds and diseases.

The current Ritigala Nature Reserve is shrouded in mystery and is made even more alluring by the silence that speaks of hidden animals, miraculous herbs and the almost total absence of tourism.

A thousand myths and legends accompany this site: one of the mysterious aspects is the belief in the existence of a herb called "Sansevi" in Sanskrit, which is thought to have the power to give long life by curing any human pain. Some texts claim that it glows in the dark and that it cures any disease. It was said that the medicines prepared with this herb could even revive a dead person.

This plant, we'd read from Nande's texts, is considered to have incredible properties by Ayurvedic medicine and has been unsuccessfully sought for centuries, right up to modern times. I remembered that Nande had often talked about this herb in his notes, but at the time I hadn't understood its potential and only after the name had emerged from the leaf of destiny did I manage to link everything together!

Everything now seemed clearer: he had handed down the leaf that was actually his, and with it the secret of the magic herb, as if it were a message for someone who needed to use it. He had tried to do so in various ways, writing it in the diaries found at Wirdana and making sure that the leaf got to his descendants.

Finding the exact place where the miraculous herb would be found was no easy task, since the only instructions were legends handed down by who knows how many rumours: getting closer to the place wouldn't have been enough. We needed help and the only real help would come from those who had lived in the area for millennia, as long as the legends: the Vedda!

I'd only vaguely heard of that tribe, which lived in the jungle located in the eastern area of the country and had the peculiar characteristic of being composed of non-sedentary hunters, who also dedicated their time to the collection of honey, roots and herbs of various kinds. The Vedda found refuge in caves or huts, built with branches or tree bark. They were divided into small groups of families or clans.

Obviously, in that period, the Vedda people were also experiencing one of most difficult times in their history. They were trying to protect their cultural roots and their heritage, so steeped in tradition, with all their might, but their demands of the government to safeguard their uniqueness often went unheeded.

The forest was everything for the Vedda: being animists, they lived in it as if it were a home, as if it were a temple for prayer, and in it they found everything they needed thanks to its medicinal herbs and hunting. Denying them the right to live *in* the forest and *with* the forest was tantamount to depriving them of the right to live as free men and, as they themselves admitted, meant they wouldn't know how to continue living. It seems that, due to the fact that they keep secrets like the miraculous herb, meeting them was not particularly easy.

They were decimated during the civil war and only a few accessible frontier villages remained; with Nande's knowledge and the hours that Channa had dedicated to research, with the help of a local guide, we were able to reach the Vedda village after a five-hour walk. It was dusk: the huts located along the sides introduced us to a scenario that I'd never seen before, it was like entering the Neolithic period.

The Vedda are very small, almost pygmies and totally different from the Sinhalese; the man we met at the entrance was the chief of the community and welcomed us with a greeting that conveyed all the pride of his people. Once again, I felt almost uncomfortable for being who I was when faced with the pride of a true tribal chief.

After a while we made an offering, as usual, and his eyes betrayed the frustration of having to accept in order to survive; a sense of sadness overwhelmed me as I looked at that little man.

As if he had always been trained in respect and local customs, fortunately Channa knew how to behave and, as had often happened to me in the past, I went with the flow without asking questions.

It was incredible how, despite being forgotten, ostracised for centuries and mutilated by civil wars and the interests of tourism, the Vedda retain a strong, tangible identity. Even though I wanted to ask a thousand questions, Channa made me understand that each of my questions would require a complex answer and that their circumstances had to be treated with extreme delicacy. If we wanted their help, we somehow had to try to create real relationships and understand the situation of such a highly delicate people.

For years, I'd been fighting against the role of the outsider, the unknown, different person, trying to belong to that land... and there, more than ever, I silently tried to mingle with their silent torment.

Channa showed him the leaf almost fearfully, obviously the chief didn't speak Sanskrit, but surprisingly he knew full well what it was, but even more surprising was when we mentioned Nande's name!

The man must have been at least eighty years old and remembered him very well: he told us that years before he had been there and had lived with them for months. That man was incredible, where hadn't he been? What hadn't he tried to find out about his traditions and his country?

All this opened the doors to his trust and the next morning, after many hours of walking, between expanses of teak and forests of maraa trees, he proudly showed us the place where the plants of "Sansevi" grew.

Channa was unbelievably excited by the sight of that infinite expanse of small plants and their prodigious leaves. We managed to collect a quantity necessary to prepare medicines and potions that would last us a long time. The Chief of the Vedda explained how to extract the precious medicine and that few on the island knew of the incredible effectiveness of those plants.

He recommended that we make good use of it and invited us to come back soon.

Back in Galle, Channa began to work on it so much that I hardly saw him anymore. He stayed in his laboratory for hours, entire days. In my mind, I saw the image of his grandfather locked inside the small colonial house, studying and preparing potions and infusions with the enthusiasm of someone who truly believes in what they're doing. I thought that they covertly shared many things and at times it really felt like I was looking at Nande.

In the meantime, I was preparing the Christmas holidays at Wirdana, to try to find some serenity and give some to those around me, who had lost everything.

CHAPTER 20

That Christmas was a quiet period: our life went by serenely, you might say; we were together and that mattered more than anything else. We had also received some bookings and the few tourists who visited Wirdana regardless of fears were the kind of people I adored: intelligent and keen to really take an interest in the country, open to listening and, above all, to trying to understand. They had arrived, despite everything, to give this people a chance; the beauty of that place and the profound culture went beyond the bombs, as well as their fears.

Their presence allowed us to return to something close to normality, which gave us hope. Guests arrived from the most disparate places on the planet, happy to travel to such a fascinating place; they travelled tens of thousands of miles to make their small contribution to this unfortunate corner of the world!

February came around; it was 2020 and although it was the best season, that year the black clouds that had gathered had not yet gone away. That day, I looked at the sky and a shiver went down my spine: in a flash, I saw everything I had been through since I had arrived in Sri Lanka and I stopped breathing for a moment, then I looked at Channa and thought that nothing could happen to me when I was by his side, but I didn't know how wrong I was, yet again.

The whole world would soon be turned upside down by something none of us could have imagined, all our certainties and dreams would be erased, swept away.

It's difficult for me to describe in a few short sentences what happened shortly thereafter, but I think history can speak for me; I'll limit myself to describing what was and was going to happen on my island. Only a partial view of the global drama.

The first news to come from Wuhan was alarming, but no one yet imagined what would happen. In a country like Sri Lanka, where ninety percent of the population is treated with Ayurveda and mortality is significantly higher than in industrialised countries, the perception of the disease was totally different. In Sri Lanka, thousands of people still die from dengue and typhoid fever every year.

That which in Europe was traumatising everyday life, had a different meaning here for various reasons and there were even some who thought that the pandemic would serve to rebalance economic differences in the hope of establishing a new social equilibrium.

The news coming from Italy was shocking, but everything still seemed so far away. The airport had immediately been closed and the island found itself totally isolated in a matter of days. Living on an island in these cases can be a good or a bad thing: obviously, you can shut everything and barricade yourself inside, but the result is complete isolation, which in the case of Sri Lanka had aggravated the gaps that already existed, cutting its ties with the rest of the world. Impositions were also strict on the island itself: the only way to survive was to block any contact between the provinces.

The consequence of doing so was a disproportionate increase in the prices of all essential goods, which had obviously aggravated an already precarious situation further. Initially, there were relatively few cases, especially compared to Western countries, but the well-founded fear was that as the number of people tested increased, the actual number of infections would prove much higher. Another problem was that, as had happened in the past, some groups in Sri Lanka were targeted and accused of spreading the virus. These groups included refugees, the poor and Muslims. The government and human rights organisations continuously called on the population to remain united, especially in such difficult times.

The government had even deployed the army to ensure that no one broke the rules, calling the fight against COVID-19 a "war" that needed to be fought together, using a term that was still very much felt by the population. The harsh and authoritarian way in which the Sri Lankan government was trying to overcome the crisis was seen by many as too extreme, but the shadow of a serious epidemic and the utter precariousness of the health system triggered frantic choices whose aim was solely that of containing the epidemic.

Despite the curfew, hospitals and shops for Ayurvedic treatments, which were also considered "essential services", remained open. The consumption of ingredients for these treatments based on coriander, ginger, turmeric and neem had increased disproportionately.

Ayurvedic medicine doctors, which included Channa, were allowed to visit and treat patients, especially those who were receiving treatment for COVID-19. Obviously, there was total chaos and no one knew what to believe or in which direction to go.

Thousands of people had defied restrictions to fight the virus by heading to a small village in central Sri Lanka, facing endless queues to buy a syrup that a self-styled guru claimed could prevent and cure the Coronavirus. Many other charlatans had taken advantage of the situation to make easy money by convincing the frightened population to gulp down anything and everything in order to save themselves.

The nation's doctors had obviously debunked the claim, pointing out that there was no scientific basis for saying that the syrup could cure or prevent the disease.

Channa began to collect the data that emerged on the relationship between Ayurvedic medicine and its use during the pandemic; in fact, our hope was that of allowing steps to be taken towards its greater use clinical and scientific fields. Ayurveda served as a supplementary element, which differed based on the severity of the cases. We came to the conclusion that Ayurveda, yoga and meditation could undoubtedly play a crucial role in enhancing preventive measures.

A good immune system is essential for the prevention of, and safeguarding against, the spread of a pandemic caused by any virus and, at that time, only high levels of immunity could act as a protective shield.

There is no scientific evidence that any of these alternative remedies can prevent or cure COVID-19, but even this claim could be taken with a grain of salt since "scientifically" is a misused term much of the time.

In another preventive move, the Sri Lankan government had prepared a plan based on Ayurvedic medicine to improve the immune system and Ayurvedic doctors and clinics were included in the early detection system. However, the warning was still that it was only a question of prevention and support.

What doctors like Channa argued was that all these treatments had no harmful effects, anyway, and they leaned towards treating COVID-19 patients becoming a kind of collaboration between Ayurvedic and Western hospitals.

In the meantime, we had begun to treat ourselves by gargling with very salty water, drinking infusions of sanjeva and coriander and inhaling infusions of guava leaves, neem leaves and whatever Nande's garden provided.

I have to admit that one of the benefits of living in a country that is so different from the one I grew up in is learning that there are many different ways of dealing with disease. I think that in our western world, we've lost the understanding that nature often gives us the remedy. We've lost the knowledge of our ancestors.

If I reflect on the fact that the death rate of COVID-19 cases treated in Ayurvedic hospitals is close to zero (although it undoubtedly depends on the fact that seriously ill patients aren't admitted), I start thinking that perhaps we're doing something wrong in the West, not in the sense of treatment, of course, but our mentality!

I'm not saying Ayurveda is the solution, but it's definitely underestimated.

As far as I can bear witness, "sanjeva" alleviated respiratory problems and proved to be a real help during convalescence, especially for the elderly who had caught the disease. Of course, it was merely of very little help, I knew that full well, but Nande's instructions once again revealed themselves as precious as ever.

However, in that fragile ecosystem, the pandemic was also upsetting other precarious equilibriums, not just those related to human health. As in the rest of the world, at the beginning the lockdown had had a positive impact on the fauna in the national parks, which had long complained about too many visitors, animals had reproduced in large numbers undisturbed and nature had breathed for a while. However, when visitors dwindled, the parks soon became an attractive hunting ground for poachers.

With no one to protect it, wildlife was more vulnerable than ever.

Some leopards, which are the symbols of the country, had been killed using traps and half the elephants had been exterminated in the last few months alone. As always happens during wars or, as we were able to see, during difficult times for man, issues concerning nature on our planet sadly doesn't seem to interest anyone.

That wasn't all: as if the raging pandemic were not enough, the greatest environmental disaster in the history of Sri Lanka was taking place at the same time off the coast of the country.

The ship, which was called the MV X-Press, had burned for thirteen days as it lay anchored about a dozen miles north of the capital Colombo, spilling nitric acid, sodium hydroxide and other dangerous chemical components into the sea and towards the beaches, as well as the contents of lots of containers of raw materials used in the production of plastic bags.

What was happening turned out to be a huge problem, not just for local fishermen, but for the entire fragile ecosystem and, consequently, for the entire population of the island.

Countless marine animals washed up on the beaches and had unsuspectingly swallowed billions of "nurdles", tiny lethal plastic balls. Hundreds of turtles, whales and dolphins paid for the umpteenth disaster caused by the wicked human neglect with their lives. Not to mention the thousands of seabirds and fish which, as happens in these cases, don't even make the news anymore.

The sea and nature remind us, they are our common belonging. It's no longer sufficient for the world to be moved by the images of devastation in Sri Lanka. Instead, the emotions that are felt need to trigger requests for a change of course.

Science and technology must be aimed in this direction and they can no longer ignore ecology. It's not too much to ask if we hope for progress that will at least free us from poisons.

Once again, poor countries like this one will be the ones to pay the highest price. I thought that we can no longer turn our heads the other way, because we cannot allow a superficial approach in a country like Sri Lanka, where at the moment there isn't even enough money to buy vaccines against the pandemic.

In order to survive, the government needs to provide concrete answers, but unfortunately the chances that the island can cope with these problems on its own are slim, especially in light of the fact that the pandemic has led to a weakening of the tourism, textile and agricultural industries.

Perhaps the hope is another: it would be enough to realise that this pandemic has shown us the fragility of an entire civilisation, its economic and health systems. Now that the hyper-specialised and hyper-technological social system of which we are a part is paralysed, I wonder whether we're able to change our vision?

Then, I think back to Nande and my indigenous friends, the Vedda, so dangerously anxious to resemble non-savages, despite not realising that right now they find themselves at a great advantage.

The forest can, as it has for thousands of years, provide them with food, shelter and medicinal herbs.

That skill has not yet vanished under the pressure of modernization. Every village elder knows where to find the right leaves to cure an infection or a snake bite and young people still know how to track footprints, find honey and work roots.

Hearing and smell are still capable of identifying prey in a dark clearing, invaded by a herb called sanjeva. For thousands of years, there has never been a lack of sustenance in those lands for every one of its inhabitants, whether man or animal.

Globalised civilisation, on the other hand, is a giant victim of its own structure! This social hive crumbles at this critical moment.

A fragile society that tends to repudiate its ties to nature or, worse, to believe that they never existed. Perhaps what's needed is a rebalancing of jobs and duties to allow new categories of extinct professionals re-emerge: skilled hunters, water seekers, good climbers, trap builders and herb finders!

After a few months, in spite of ourselves, we were forced to leave Sri Lanka like many other "outsiders", since the situation had worsened. Staying there would no longer be safe, especially for me; Channa decided to go with me, knowing that we would be back as soon as possible, even though we didn't know what would actually happen.

When I said goodbye to Nirosh and my boys, I knew it would be a long time before I could see them again. Nirosh said goodbye with his sweet smile: "Take care madam, stay safe". Once again, they were thinking of me, without even knowing how they themselves would survive.

I was leaving Wirdana and my beloved dogs, who had become my friends.

After six years of hopes and dreams, I left what had become my world. After battles won and lost, after having fought with every sinew to make my way in a hostile, but equally wonderful world, I understood that something stronger than me had won, for now.

Everything that had happened had upset all the equilibriums that I had created with so much effort and I had to leave for now.

I gave thanks for every single moment spent on my island, moments that had taught and given me so much. I thanked fate for taking me there and for giving me this invaluable opportunity. I knew it wasn't a goodbye, I knew that my bond with that land would be indissoluble.

We left on a day in April, when the weather was still mild and humidity permeated you to the core, just like when it all started; nature was still there, lush and powerful, as if trying to pretend nothing had happened.

Flying over the places I had loved so much, I thought with regret that I had not yet finished my task, but what made me suffer most was not having been able to do enough for that island and the sad knowledge that no one would help that country, unless it was to make it even more economically dependent.

However, as the leaf of fate had foretold, I left with a different awareness.

It's impossible to get out of such an apocalypse today and return to life as it was before, putting everything we experienced behind us. Above all, it's not possible because what happened to us opened our eyes to the tragedies to which we expose ourselves, using creation, as we've done until now, not to preserve and improve it, but to obtain everything that satisfies our selfish, immediate ends, without limits. It has also exposed the immeasurable value of people, sometimes exalting it through solidarity, other times wounding it due to inequalities.

It's made us understand that the common good depends in good part on those who govern, undoubtedly, but it depends just as much on each of us.

As far as I was concerned, with the help of Nande, the old "guardian of the fireflies", I hoped that I had at least made a small contribution. That had to be the case, because only then would everything I had experienced not have been in vain.

If you ever happen to visit this little corner of the world, perhaps you could take a trip to the locations in my story, so you can experience Nande's places and see where I went on my adventures, but above all you can to get to know Sri Lanka and its incredible people that, now more than ever, deserves to be encouraged to build a new future after so much suffering.

If you happen, in a better future, to go all the way out there, I hope you'll still find what I found: one of the most fascinating places on earth.

AUTHOR'S NOTE

The story in this book is partly fictional, but the places and characters are all real. They're wonderful people without whom I could never have written this and without whom building my paradise would have been impossible.

I'd like to thank Nande, of course, who was a real person and helped me learn the secrets of Ayurveda, thank Nirosh, who is still my right-hand man in my business today, thank Sam, who after having built Wirdana manages his own non-profit organisation and continues his trade as a builder, thank Tulsie and Emil, Sampatha and my fantastic guys, who work every day, even now, so that Wirdana can survive together with this beautiful country.

Above all, I'd like to thank my husband, Channa, for having been with me for better or for worse!

AYURVEDIC HERBS

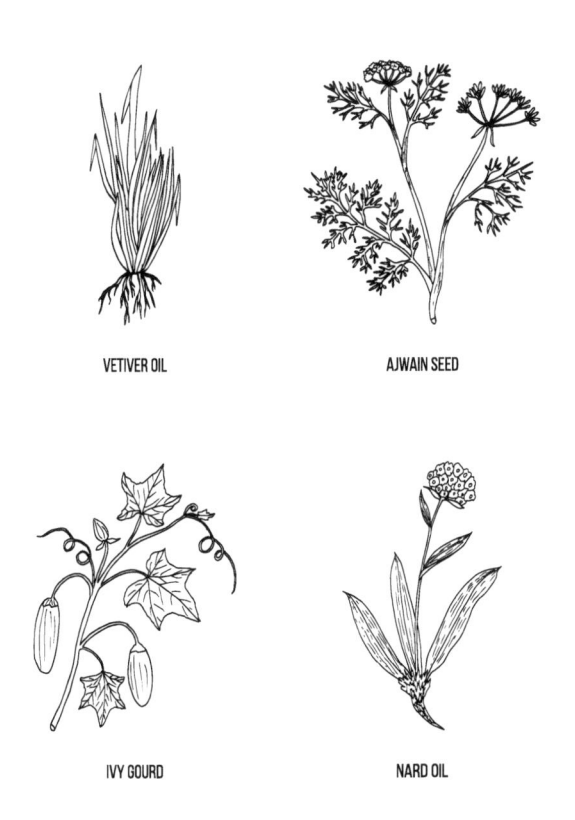

VETIVER OIL

AJWAIN SEED

IVY GOURD

NARD OIL

PIPPALI

LOTUS

SATAVARI

NONI

ACORUS CALAMUS

SANDALWOOD OIL

NEEM

CARDAMOM

BITTER MELON

HOLY BASIL

BACOPA

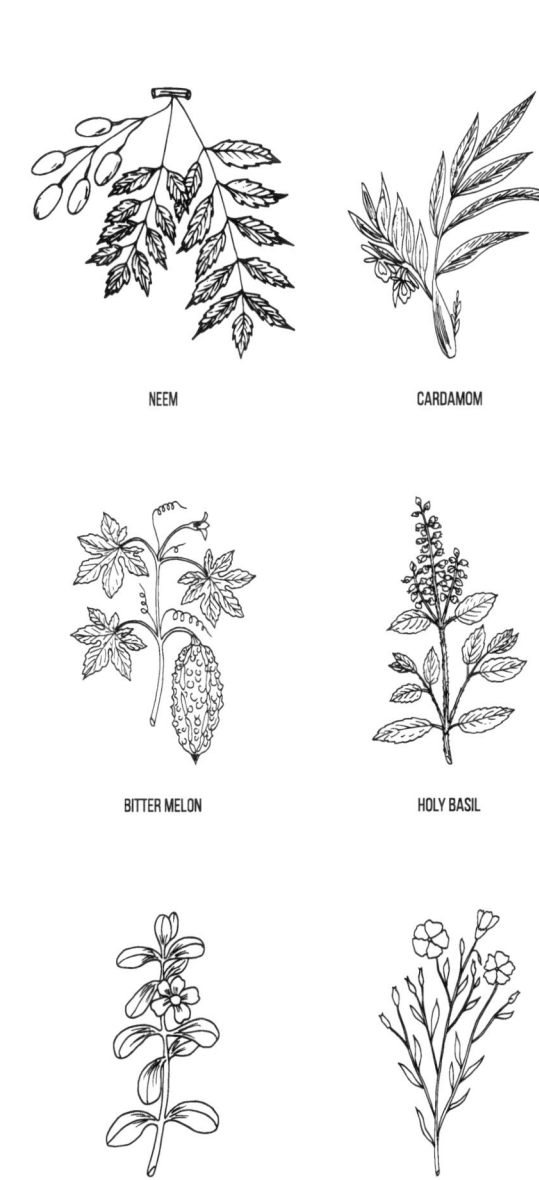

FLAX SEED

Printed by Amazon Italia Logistica S.r.l.
Torrazza Piemonte (TO), Italy